This is a work of fiction. Names, characters, places, and incidents either are the product of the author's imagination or are used fictitiously. Any resemblance to actual persons, living or dead, events, or locales is entirely coincidental.

Copyright © Jennifer Corvid, 2021 All rights reserved.

No part of this book may be reproduced in any form by an electronic or mechanical means, including information storage and retrieval systems, without permission in writing from the publisher, except by a reviewer who may quote brief passages in a review.

Cover art by Andrew Herman

ISBN 978-1-008-90788-1

IMAGO

Chapter One: The Hand-Off	1
Chapter Two: The Cargo	4
Chapter Three: Home	9
Chapter Four: Safehouse	13
Chapter Five: Magpie	17
Chapter Six: Family	22
Chapter Seven: Shootout	28
Chapter Eight: Questions	32
Chapter Nine: Catching Up	36
Chapter Ten: Call to Arms	39
Chapter Eleven: Collision	42
Chapter Twelve: Journey	50
Chapter Thirteen: The City of Snakes	54
Chapter Fourteen: Corpse Orchard	61
Chapter Fifteen: Beneath the Sands	64
Chapter Sixteen: Paradise Found	72
Chapter Seventeen: The Great Beast	76
Chapter Eighteen: Ascension	82
Chapter Nineteen: Genesis	90
Epilogue	97

Chapter One: The Hand-Off

Even through the filters of my respirator, the noxious air of the city stung my throat and lungs with every breath. The miasma of waste and decay pulsed with the tide, fresh bursts of rot rushing in with every crashing wave. I checked my watch, the illuminated face reading twelve fifteen. "Late," I sighed, "Nothing new there." My line of work took me here often, the water was one of the only ways to smuggle contraband these days, and even then it wasn't easy. Searchlights moved along the horizon, attached to gunships prepared to blow any unauthorized vessel to rubble. The fleshy masses just below the surface bobbed horribly with the tide. Their pathetic limbs writhed ineffectually, just barely shifting their corpulent forms. The campaign to introduce them to our waters called them Sweepers, but most people who didn't make the conscious decision to ignore them entirely called them Shit Eaters. The posters painted them as cartoonish mascots of a greener tomorrow, grinning amphibious things that would passively clean up our seas. Their all-too-human faces had been notably absent from the push to release them publicly. I locked eyes with one as it fought helplessly against the tide, webbed bony fingers flailing under the surface. There was no understanding there, they lacked the vital essence that made something truly human, but there was a distinct sense that it was pleading with me. Its jaw split as it released its mournful song, the whale-like maw far too large for the human face above it, lined with baleen to help it pick plastic from the water. The microbiome in its gut would help it break down the material, though a friend who had helped in engineering the creatures entrusted to me on a drunken night that the process of digestion was still agony for the things.

My attention snapped from the Sweeper to the hand rising from the water and pulling itself up the dock. "Little help?" A voice came as a second hand and a head broke the surface. I reached for it and pulled my contact to the surface. He was tall, slender, carrying a bloodsoaked harpoon gun on his hip, and dressed in a black spandex suit and helmet. His arms and feet were uncovered, revealing the pale blue scales, webbed digits and talons typical of his kind. The merfolk had a reputation as criminals, most had opted to undergo the change to aid in smuggling, though others simply found joy in exploring depths no natural human ever could. Arnie was certainly of the former category. He unhooked the waterproof carrier from his back, taking it under his arm and raising a clawed hand to me. "You got the cash?"

"What, you don't trust me?" I smirked, though the respirator obscured it.

"I've been fucked before."

"By me?"

"Not yet. Y'know how it is, the second someone gets on your good side is the second they stab you in the gills."

"Fair enough," I shrugged, handing off the briefcase, "It should all be there." He took a moment to count through stacks of bills inside, then nodded slowly.

"Alright," he began to open the carrier, "Pleasure doing business with you." He pulled out the bizarre object in his care, passing it to me before hastily shoving the briefcase into his carrier and diving back into the water. My eyes met the

Sweeper again, but it had turned away from me now. A thick carapace was spreading across its ribs. Early stages of the crustacean plague. I struggled to look away from the creature as I packed the cargo into my carrier. I knew in the morning a handler would likely notice the infection, if they didn't then its implants would certainly pick up on it soon, and it would be euthanized to prevent further spread. *A shame,* I thought, *it would have probably been happier this way.*

Chapter Two: The Cargo

The click of the airlock behind me told me it was safe to remove my respirator. I sat the carrier down in the motel closet and stripped, the foul odour lingering on the clothes until the moment the washer's door closed on them. The shower came stocked with an assortment of fragranced shampoos and body washes, and I'll admit that I relished in the thought of smelling like something other than pollution or chemical detergents for a change. The strong apple scent that followed me even after I dried off and changed was slightly overpowering, though it was preferable to the stench outside the door. Fresh air was pumped in by the oxygen cyclers, giving the room a distinct sterility. I settled into the well worn armchair in the corner of the room and pulled my cargo from its carrier. It was a strange contraption. I had smuggled everything from drugs, to illegal implants, to disembodied heads awaiting transplant. This was closest to the latter, but distinctly different. A metal cylinder with small glass windows, filled with an opaque orange fluid. The shadow of an amorphous thing peered through the small openings, but it didn't seem to move unless the container was disturbed. I had seen brains, or neuroplastic constructs at least, transported in similar vessels, but they had one key difference; They had a built in oxygen supply, usually a small tank of compressed air, just enough for the journey and a small margin of error. This was something else, an oxygen cycler. It was small, cobbled together, likely only providing the absolute bare minimum, but it was built for a long stay. Brains would never be kept in something like this, too many organizations fighting for their rights. No sensory inputs, anything inside would have to be sedated for the duration or it would go mad in its blind, deaf, touchless abyss. I couldn't do anything about it. My job was simple: pickup, transport and delivery. I didn't get to ask questions, and quite frankly I knew I wouldn't want the answers.

I packed away the cylinder in its carrier, glancing over the contact details of the group who'd contracted me. "The Church of the Divine Reconciliation." There was an attached number, though it had been hand-scrawled across the card with the original number crossed out. Large underlined letters read "**IN CASE OF EMERGENCIES ONLY**."

"What the hell have I gotten myself into this time," I shook my head, fiddling instinctively with the hedgehog in my pocket. My gloved thumb ran along the bristles and I pulled it from its place. The grip was cold, metallic and heavy in my hand. The barrel was warm, pink and ridged. A small black eye trained itself directly forward, its spines angled in the direction of its gaze. The slightest pressure on the trigger and it would hurl the venomous quills at whatever it was pointed at, killing them in seconds. I had never had to fire it, thankfully. Usually the sight of a hedgehog is enough to de-escalate the conflict. It's an awful way to die.

My attention snapped away from the fleshy firearm as the bell sounded at my door. I returned it to my jeans as the quills retracted, but made a point to keep a grip on the handle. I looked at the small viewport showing a live feed of the man on the other side of the door. He was short, broad, scarred, and beet red. Even through his respirator I could see he wore a deep scowl, and I knew why.

"I know you're in there Tiff, open the damn door." He shouted loud enough to peak the mic. I paused, waiting to see if he'd leave given a lack of response. "Listen, you bitch," no such luck, "You open this goddamn door and give me my money, or so help me I'll blow it down and gut you!" My hand remained fast on the hedgehog, its quills rustling with anticipation. The image on the monitor made it clear he wasn't bluffing, two of his goons flanked him on either side, modified almost beyond recognition as humans. One was so unfathomably bulky that his shoulders almost seemed to swallow his neck, his hands were each big enough to wrap completely around a head and crush it like an overripe peach. The other was all edges, blades and bones jutted horrifically from him, tearing through the pinstripe suit that wouldn't look out of place in an old gangster movie. The contrast between the monstrous henchmen and their portly, puny boss only served to make them seem more intimidating. Xander Maxwell was well known in the criminal underworld, fancying himself something of a kingpin. I knew he wasn't here for the money, not really, for him that was chump change. He was here because I hurt his pride. The male ego is a fragile thing, and it doesn't cope well with being left chained to a bed naked, beaten senseless as someone robs you blind. It has particular trouble when that comes from a woman.

I grabbed the carrier and slung it over my shoulder, slid my respirator into place and shifted my hedgehog to my left hand. As much as Maxwell had it coming, he wasn't worth the added heat that comes with a murder charge. I slipped the stun baton out of my boot and extended it, sparks discharging as its telescopic form unfolded. Maxwell made a gesture to the burlier of his two goons, who responded with a nod. His whole body rippled as he reared back and hurled his bulk toward the airlock. I slammed the door control, causing the behemoth to stumble awkwardly against the unexpected emptiness and smash hard into the floor. Maxwell gestured to the other henchman, who dashed in through the open doorway and collided full force with my stun baton. I stepped over him as he dropped to the floor and focused my hedgehog on Maxwell's glimmering forehead.

"Take one step toward me," I growled, "And I plant a quill in your frontal lobe." He raised his hands in surrender and took a few clumsy steps backward before bumping against a railing. "Get the hell out of my way, if I see you again I won't give you the courtesy of a warning."

"I'm sorry, I- I wasn't thi-" his eyes focused on the room behind me, "Wasn't thinking... I... Get her, Bozo!" I spun on my heels, hedgehog still trained on Maxwell's sweat-drenched forehead, just in time to see the bulkier goon had risen to his feet. I got a chance to have a better look at him then, and wish I hadn't. His legs were utterly tiny compared to his ballooned upper body, rippling with muscles I couldn't identify or safely say had been a part of him originally. His eyes were small, round and recessed, little black pits in his skull. Any trace of a nose was gone, replaced with reptilian slits that flared as he growled at me. His mouth was wide, lined with perfectly straight, flat teeth. The line between his teeth could probably be used as a ruler. All this went through my head in the half a second it took him to lunge at me. I held out the baton and closed my eyes, prepared for the worst.

Nothing.

Absolutely nothing. I opened my eyes and looked around, needing a moment to get my bearings. I was in the parking lot of the motel, the cold, stinking air hit me all at once like a brick. I heard screams and yelling, looking over I saw the silhouette of Maxwell and his goons cast against the light of my open doorway.

"What the fuck?!" Maxwell howled, "Where the fuck did she go?!"

"My arm," the bulkier one's voice was so deep and mournful it sounded like a whale song, "She took my arm." I glanced at the ground behind me and jumped back in shock, the still twitching appendage having followed me on my sudden relocation. I stifled a gasp, not wanting to be noticed and saving questions until I could say I was safe. After a second I realized that whatever had dragged me out of danger had planted me only a few feet from my bike. I sped off into the night, heading for home.

Chapter Three: Home

The bike squealed to halt in the early rays of sunlight peering through dark, toxic clouds. I had spent the hours-long drive considering what had happened at the motel. Maxwell's goons were likely to find me again soon, and the arm would only serve to fuel their bloodlust. I couldn't stay home long, I knew that as I walked up the decrepit stairway to my apartment. I still couldn't account for what had happened at the motel, not completely. I'd heard rumors of teleportation, but the rumors made two things clear. It wasn't instant, and it wasn't suitable for organics. Didn't help that it took a rig the size of a warehouse on either end to pull it off. The thoughts of the impossible thing I'd experienced faded from my mind as I laid a hand on the doorknob. I made a point to be quiet as I turned it.

"Babe," I whispered into the dark room, "Babe, you up?"

The mechanical crackle of her speakers came before the words, "Tiff! I wasn't expecting you back for hours, did something happen?" I flipped the light on and approached Beth's tank, settling into the chair beside her.

"Yeah, Xander Maxwell decided to show up at the motel."

"He did? Did he hurt you?"

"No, not for lack of trying though. I came back to grab some stuff, I'm gonna have to call Frankie to get you somewhere safe until I can deal with this mess."

"I thought you said you killed him last time you ran into him." There was a note of disappointment in her voice, I remembered the look that used to come with that tone. Puppy dog eyes and a pout that would almost make a girl ashamed to have let someone live. Now I was just met with the wet, bloody folds of grey matter in a tank and a single expressionless eye on a mechanical arm.

"I said I left him for dead. Bastard bled so much his white sheets turned red, I didn't think he'd survive that."

"Hmph," she sighed, though the crackle of her synthetic voice almost swallowed the sound. I laid a hand on the tactile disc wired to her, stroking it gently.

"Don't worry, I'll make sure I kill the son of a bitch next time. I promise."

The water in her tank bubbled and a laugh escaped the tinny speaker. Even without a body, she had a bloodthirsty streak to her that was strangely endearing.

"Do you mind if we…" her words trailed off as a small panel on her cabinet slid open and a long, grey wire poked out. I nodded to her, unfastening the steel cap on my neck.

"I think we have some time."

I plugged her jack into the port on my neck and saw myself looking down at her, from the perspective of her eye.

Close your eyes, she thought, *I don't like seeing myself like this.*

Sorry, I closed my eyes, and she closed hers. The blackness was quickly replaced by the bright lights and joyous sounds of a carnival. People wandered by, memories of people, smiling and laughing, eating cotton candy, not a respirator or cloud of smog in sight.

I wish we could go back here, her voice came from behind me, *do you think we can? Someday?* I turned to look at her. Not the mass of tissue in a nutrient slurry that she'd come to be, I looked at her as she was that night. A denim jacket over a black dress, boots that could crush a man's head, long black hair that refused to be tamed. She was beautiful. She reached a hand to me and I instinctively pulled back, afraid to shatter the illusion. *It's okay,* she smiled patiently, *I can hang on this time.* I felt the warmth of her touch for the first time in months, and didn't even think before I pulled her into an embrace.

I missed you, I blurted out.

You see me everyday, Tiff, she laughed.

I miss holding you. I miss touching your hair. I miss how you smell.

I can imagine this is a little better than the formaldehyde stink out there, she giggled.

So much better, I smiled with my face buried in her neck, *what should we do? Ferris whe-* I recoiled as I saw her face. She raised a hand to it and turned away.

Fuck, she screamed, the carnival fell away and left us in a white void, *I'm sorry, fuck, shit.* Her body twisted and warped, eventually dissolving to static. Her blurred silhouette turned back to me. *I'm so sorry,* she sobbed, *I really thought I could keep it together this time.*

It's o-

"-kay," My eyes adjusted to the poorly lit apartment as they fluttered open, ripped violently from the simulation.

"I'm sorry," she repeated, the jack retracting into its compartment. "Maybe you should just go, I'll call Frankie. The sooner you get this delivery done, the sooner we can get back to some kind of normal."

"Beth," I laid my hand on her tactile disc, "It's okay. I'm not mad. We don't have to plug in, we can just watch a movie like the old days."

"You're sure?" She sounded on the verge of tears, though she couldn't really cry anymore.

"I'm sure. I'll call Frankie and have him take you to a safehouse by morning, until then I'm not going anywhere. Okay?"

"Okay."

"Now, who's turn is it to pick the movie again?" I smiled into her eye.

Chapter Four: Safehouse

Frankie and I had to lift Beth's cabinet into the back of his van with a tarp over her. The bulk of her life support systems weren't exactly conducive to transport, and she occupied most of the floorspace once she was inside. I uncovered her eye so she could see and sat opposite her, Frankie in the driver's seat on the other side of the mesh grating.

"I really appreciate you doing this for us, Frank," Beth crackled.

"No problem," his mandibles worked awkwardly around the words. His rigid face gave little away and his voice was so distorted that it couldn't be parsed for any subtle meaning, but before the crustacean plague had claimed his ability to emote I always knew him to be quite jovial.

"Seriously man, I hate to put you out like this, I feel like I'm taking advantage of you," I yelled through the grate.

"It's not a big deal, really. You two are practically family, I know if the tables were turned I could rely on you." He was right, of course. He didn't need to phrase it hypothetically, he'd often got on someone's bad side and stowed away with me. "Just do me a favor and kill that Maxwell prick before he gets the bright idea to make me the day's special at some seafood joint," his mouthparts rustled in some approximation of a laugh.

"Don't you worry, Frankie," I tightened my grip on the hedgehog, "Next time I see the bastard he's as good as dead."

"I love when you do that," Beth laughed.

"Do what?"

"Grip that peashooter when you're talking all serious, we both know you've never actually fired it. Poor thing, probably feels underutilized."

"Don't tell me she's playing with that porcupine again," Frankie yelled from the driver's seat.

"Hedgehog!" I countered, perhaps a little do defensively, drawing a chuckle out of Beth.

"Whatever, just don't mess with that thing in my van! They have a mind of their own and I don't feel like gettin' pumped full of more venom than an all-pufferfish buffet."

"Don't worry," Beth sighed, "They only get like that with trigger-happy owners. Firing gets a little too reflexive. Hers probably wouldn't go off if she did pull the trigger."

"Whatever, they're still illegal, just put it away before we get pulled over."

"Fine," I sighed, before muttering "Buzzkill" under my breath.

"I heard that." Frankie shook his head. "Whatever, doesn't matter. We're here." The van pulled up to an inconspicuous warehouse and Frankie held his phone to the hole in his carapace where his ear used to be. He muttered a few words down the line in french and the large door in front of us opened.

"Oh god," Beth groaned, "Don't tell me *they're* here." I understood the implication immediately and felt sorry for Beth as I heard Frankie's approximation of a laugh again.

"I'm afraid they are," Frankie rasped, "Sorry, you're not the only ones lying low at the moment."

The van screeched to a halt and the door closed behind us, swallowing the room in darkness. I opened the door, braced to hear Beth's audible disgust.

"Tiffany! Bethany! My two favourite ladies! How are we on this fine morning, eh?" They stood with open arms, a goofy grin plastered on their face with a trickle of blood rolling down their chin. An oversized coat hung on their lanky frame and their eyes shone with a blue luminescence in the dark warehouse.

"Hello, Claude," Beth's voice dripped with disdain, not that Claude seemed to notice or care.

"So we're going to be roomies for a few days, is that so? I look forward to recounting stories of my many escapades since last we met!" They gestured with a manic glee that made me grin, not that I'd let Beth know. I had always been a bit more fond of Claude than her, though admittedly that may have something to do with our… History.

"I'm sure she'd love to hear it, pal," I laid a hand on the plasmavore's shoulder and gripped tight enough to get their attention, "But she's just had a rough journey, you know how she gets. Maybe give her a day or two before you lay into her with the escapades." I locked eyes with them and tightened my grip a little more, their lips retracting in pain to show six metallic fangs.

"Ah, oui, of course," they pulled away from my grip with a serpentine fluidity, "I'll give her some time to rest."

"You do that," I turned back to Beth, who Frankie had almost finished unloading from the van, "You gonna be okay here?"

"Yeah," her voice came in a staticky whisper, "I think I'll be just fine. Just stay safe and don't forget to call. And make sure you're eating, I don't want to worry about you wasting away on me."

"I'll be fine, babe," I ran my fingers in a circle on her tactile disc, "I promise."

Chapter Five: Magpie

The sun hung high over New Babylon City, but its light was dim through the thick clouds that smothered it. Faint neon billboards and the orange glow of streetlamps did more to illuminate the harsh concrete towers on all sides. It would be at least three days to get to the drop off point, maybe more if I had any more run-ins with Maxwell's men. My bike weaved between the traffic, reacting to objects on the road with little input from me. I reached into my pocket for the card with my contact's number, hoping to find some other hint I missed about what exactly I was carrying. I'd gotten whole families across borders in a bag full of neuro-cylinders and it hadn't had a fraction of a payout like this, WMDs didn't even hit these figures. I remembered the words on its face. The Church of the Divine Reconciliation, another cult that had sprung up in the last few years. Most were just luddites or reactionaries that wanted to bring mankind back to what we used to be before the implants and gene-mods. Not the Reconcilers. They had a different vision for the world, they thought that technology was the way forward. That man could become divine. It was out there, sure, but the people who believed it were the sort of power hungry narcissists with the desire to see it happen and the influence to see it through. It's no mystery why their church had risen to the position it had, or how they could throw this sort of cash towards some lowlife smuggler like it was nothing.

  I snapped from the train of thought as I realized the card wasn't in my pocket. "Fuck!" I shouted, confident that my engine and my respirator would muffle the sound enough to not draw much attention. The card was still at the motel. Maxwell had probably found it, he knew where I was going.

I picked up speed, suddenly acutely aware of the massive bullseye on my back. Maxwell might have been a pathetic cretin, but he also had money, the kind of money that buys muscle. There wasn't a hope in hell that I was going to be safe in the city, I decided I'd take a less direct route. The tires squealed as I made a hard turn and headed for the outskirts.

The slums were every bit the pit of despair that New Babylon was, but they weren't afraid to admit it. Maxwell's influence didn't extend out this far, this was Magpie territory. Ulysses Magpie was a lot of things. A leader, a killer, and one of the few men I shared mutual respect with. I knew I was safe here, well, as safe as anyone else was in the slums. The streets were lined with garbage, most bags had been torn open and rummaged through. The people here lived like racoons, crowded into undersized dens, starved and ravenous. The wealthy never dared set foot here. It was a place overrun by the downtrodden and desperate, and wealth wasn't a symbol of status in a place like this. It was a mark of the guilty.

Turning a corner, I was forced to brake so hard I nearly flew from my seat. A crowd stood in the road, a militia, armed to the teeth and wearing beaked masks.

"Off the cycle," one of them boomed, a bombardier's gleaming carapace shining in his bandaged hand. Not eager to be on the receiving end of its spray, I dismounted.

"Damn, did Magpie really roll out the red carpet for little old me?" I laughed.

"Silence." Another voice came from behind the raggedy crowd, dispersing them with nothing but her words and carving a path forward.

"You look… Familiar. Do I know you?" The resemblance was uncanny.

"No," she pulled a trigger and I felt a tranquilizer dart pierce my chest, my vision fading to black as she stood over me, "I'm new."

I peeled my face from the puddle of drool quickly accumulating on the table. My head was still fuzzy from the tranq, but I snapped to focus when my gaze landed on the blurry figure opposite me. She tilted her head and looked away from the gun she was polishing.

"Ah, you're awake."

"God, could you have used a more cliche line?"

"... I'm going to pretend you didn't say that, and we'll start over. Good morning, sleep well?"

"I've slept better, whatever you gave me was pretty light stuff."

"Ha. Perhaps I'll find something more to your taste next time I need to drug you."

"Please do, I can get you in touch with some dealers."

"Cute."

"Taken, sorry."

"Pity," she sighed, "Do you know why you're here?"

"Because you drugged me and dragged me here?"

"And do you know why I did that?"

"Well I'm really hoping you're gonna throw me a surprise party, but nine times out of ten that's not what happens."

"You were trespassing."

"What? No, get Magpie, he'll-"

"Ulysses Magpie is dead."

I snapped to attention. "He is? Oh… Oh god, when, how?"

"Four years ago, in his sleep."

"God, I had no idea."

"I can tell. Now, why were you in Magpie territory?"

"I was… I was making a delivery, cut through to avoid Maxwell's goons, I-" My vision blurred as tears welled up in my eyes, "Magpie's dead."

"I didn't think you'd be so upset," there was a genuine confusion in her voice, she settled back in her seat, "I didn't see you at the funeral."

"I didn't know. I haven't talked to Mags since-" The sound of a gunshot rang out in my head, still echoing all those years later. Then another. I reached for my shoulder instinctively, but my hand halted, chained to the table. I remembered the pool of red, seeping from Magpie's feathers. I remembered the sound of footsteps, the sound of my cowardice. I'd heard he recovered, but I couldn't bear to look at him again, not after leaving him.

"Well," her ebony feathers rustled as she adjusted herself uncomfortably, "I'm sorry you had to find out this way, Tiff."

I looked her in the eyes, struggling to place her. It clicked like a jigsaw in my mind. "Mel?"

Her eyes went wide at the sound of her name on my lips. Melanie Magpie. She'd changed a lot since I last saw her, the beak, the feathers, all new additions, but it was definitely her.

"Everyone just calls me Magpie these days. Ever since Dad... Yeah."

"It's good to see you," I blinked a tear from my eyes.

"You too, sis. You too."

Chapter Six: Family

"So you're running the gang now, huh?" We strolled through the streets, the people's eyes filled with fear and respect as they settled on Magpie. Her dark feathers gleamed under the streetlights like a sea of precious gems.

"More or less," she sighed, "It's not what it used to be. Dad was a pillar of the community. He united people. I'm… Not that. Most of the members stayed loyal, others left for greener pastures, a considerable handful… Well…" Gunshots rang out as if to emphasize her point, "A considerable handful would like to instil… New leadership."

"A mutiny?" I asked, and Magpie chuckled.

"I would've gone with 'coup,' you make it sound like we're pirates," she glanced at my outfit and produced as thoughtful an approximation of a scowl she could with her avian features, "I suppose you probably would think that way."

"Hey, I'm a smuggler, not a pirate! I get seasick!"

"Ha, of course. Explains why you haven't gotten your gills yet."

"You think I'd do that to myself? Have you been to the dock lately? The air is bad enough, I have absolutely no intention of breathing the water. Besides, those Sweeper things, they bother me."

"Sweepers?" She cocked her head to the side.

"Shit Eaters," I sighed.

"Ah. Yes, I suppose they aren't exactly a pleasant sight." She nodded, feigning understanding.

"It's messed up. I know they don't feel like we do but… They look so human."

"I know I'm probably not the person to ask this, but what the hell humans have you been hanging around with?" She ran a clawed hand through her feathers.

"It's their faces! And their creepy hands. They look too human, and they look like they're in pain."

"They probably are. Their diet consists entirely of plastic and they only have a shelf life of a half dozen years."

"And you don't see anything wrong with that?"

"My concern is my people," she sighed, "I don't have time for sub-sapient waste disposal drones. Anyway, we're here."

I glanced at the sign above the door. "Lenny's?" I read aloud, "Not little Lenny Herman?"

"Well, we don't call him 'little' these days, but yeah." I followed her through the airlock and removed my respirator. The chemical shower removed any trace of the miasma that lingered on fabric and feathers, but dried rapidly.

As the door to the pub opened I was overwhelmed by a new odour. Freshly cooked food, the kind of family meal I hadn't experienced in over a decade, and the powerful aroma of an assortment of alcoholic drinks. The air was filled with the sounds of casual chatter and laughter.

"You took me to a bar?"

"I did shoot you, figured I owed you a drink after that." As she spoke my hand instinctively moved to the small puncture wound where the tranq had broken my skin.

"Ha, guess I need to let you shoot me more often," we settled into the seats at the bar and a young man rose up from behind it. His hair had thinned out to the point of almost baldness and his face was lined with peculiar seams, but his boyish features and diminutive size betrayed his identity.

"Lenny," Magpie's beak twisted into a smirk, "How's business?"

"Can't complain, can't complain," He eyed me, his face warping into a look of confusion, writhing slightly at the seams, "Taking in another stray?" Magpie laughed.

"C'mon, you don't recognize her?"

His eyes pulsed strangely in their sockets before recognition entered them, "Tiff! Oh my god, I'm so sorry! You look great, doing something new with your hair?"

It was shorter than when I'd last seen him, but I got a feeling that's not what he was referring to. "I went blonde for a while, y'know, laying low. When I went back to normal the gene sculpt didn't take," I ran a hand along the streak of white in my hair, "I decided I may as well keep it. It's a nice look."

"Definitely. Anyway, can I get you ladies anything to drink?"

"The usual," Magpie said, laying down a few notes on the bartop, "And whatever she wants."

"Something sweet, I'm not picky," I smiled.

"Alrighty," he nodded, taking the money and vanishing again under the counter.

"So tell me, what did you mean by not calling him 'Little' anymore?"

"Did you not notice?"

"Notice what?"

She gestured for me to look behind her, Lenny stood at another table, taking orders.

"Okay, and?"

She gestured again, at another table. He was carrying food to them, a third arm growing from his stomach to facilitate the plates. My eyes scanned the room, noticing at least four more distinct Lennys.

"What, he's cloning himself?" I whispered.

"Look at their feet." I noticed the trails almost as soon as I'd processed the words. The floor was criss-crossed with fleshy tendrils connecting all of the Lennys, more of the meaty vines running along the walls, on the ceiling and crossing in and out of pipes around the room.

"What the fuck…"

"Admiring the view?" Lenny popped up from behind the bar again, laughing as I jumped back. "Nah, I'm just messing with you. You were looking at the connections, right?"

"Yeah, sorry," I nodded, embarrassed a little at my shock.

"Hey, don't worry about it," His tone was as jovial and nonchalant as it had been since I entered the bar. "I know it's pretty extreme, even by slum standards. Started out with an extra pair of hands to help around the kitchen, then a little more range on them, next thing you know," he unfurled his arm, splitting along the seams into a mass of squirming tendrils, "I'm spread across the whole building and need to prune myself daily so I don't start overflowing."

"Prune?" I asked, trying not to look at him as a mass of tendrils only imitating the shape of the boy I once knew.

"Y'know, a snip here, a snip there, just to keep everything tidy. At least there's no shortage of fresh meat," He laughed, "Speaking of, can I get you anything to eat? Burger's great."

"I'm vegetarian," And I had never been quite as comfortable saying it out loud as at that moment.

"Aw, shoot. You hungry, Mags?"

"I could eat."

"Alright, shouldn't be too long at all. Oh, and your drinks," A disembodied hand rose up from behind the bar with a tray and laid it down in front of us. "A bottle of whiskey and an Apple Atom Bomb." The latter was a pitcher full of a slightly phosphorescent emerald liquid, carrying an unmistakable and powerful apple scent. As Lenny once again dissolved below the bar I took a mouthful of the drink, Magpie doing the same with her bottle.

"Holy shit," I coughed, "This is strong."

"You told him you're not picky, it's a miracle he didn't give you hot sauce and vodka. That stuff is probably mostly alcohol."

"Yeah, I can tell." I winced slightly as I took another mouthful, considering that this would probably be much more palatable as shots. "What did he mean earlier, about you taking in strays?"

"Oh, that," Magpie stared down the neck of her bottle, "Y'know, there are always the unfortunates. Kids with nowhere else to go. Now, especially after the whole exodus, we have a lot of spare beds and can use the extra hands."

"You really take after him, huh?"

"This is different. For a start, I'm not renaming any of them, and I'm not asking them to call me mom. Dad didn't think you were some stray."

"No, but that's what I was, wasn't I?" I drank another mouthful of the glowing cocktail. Magpie's silence spoke volumes. She tipped the bottle and let it pour into her beak.

"Tiff," She took a breath, "You are my sister. You're my sister, and I lo-"

"Crabs!" Lenny's voice came from everywhere at once, "We got crabs!"

"Shit," Magpie pulled her gun from its holster, I followed suit with my hedgehog.

"Woah," Lenny burst up from the ground, half formed, and put my hand down, "Put that damned thing away. If I get hit with that, this whole place comes down!"

"Tiff, holster it," Magpie instructed.

Lenny's other selves ushered patrons out the back, assisting children with their respirators and funneling them into the airlocks as quickly as possible. A few stayed, drawing their weapons and moving to protect Magpie. Deep voices rumbled from outside, then the ticking started. A wall of flesh rose up to shield us, but Lenny's body splintered back into meaty particles as the wall was blown in.

The dust began to settle, and the silhouettes of four armored figures loomed in the gaping hole they had made. A cancer guard. The leader raised an arm, and I saw the faint glow of a plasma pistol charging.

"Tiffany Rose, Xander Maxwell sends his regards."

Chapter Seven: Shootout

The blast was aimed squarely for my heart, but fleshy appendages pulled me aside with such speed that I only received a scorched shoulder. I was thankful that the searing heat of the plasma bolt cauterized the wound, leaving only a crater of charred muscle visible through the hole in my jacket.

"Mags, don't tell me you brought her here with a bounty on her head," Lenny yelled from another body, tackling one of the crabs to the ground while he dragged me behind the bar.

"Jesus," Magpie yelled as she unloaded shots at the armored horde, "I didn't think she'd have crabs on her, Len."

"What in god's name did you do to Maxwell that he's willing to hire out a cancer guard?" Lenny asked me, tending to my wound. I hissed reflexively as he poured alcohol into it.

"Would you believe me if I said I didn't know?" His face made the answer clear, "He pissed off some people, me included, I took him out for drinks, took him home, pulled out some cuffs and he didn't bat an eye until I kneed him in the crotch. Beat him to a pulp and cleared out his apartment."

"Remind me to never get on your bad side," Lenny grimaced at the image in his mind. "What the fuck did he do that pissed you off that bad?"

"Let's just say I did some volunteer work on behalf of his HR department, a lot of women with a lot of complaints." Another plasma blot whizzed through the air, burning a hole in the ceiling. One of the crabs yelped in pain. A misfire, one was shot. I pulled the stun baton from my boot and extended it, sparks flying. I threw myself over the bar, landing at one of the crab's feet and bringing the arcing steel up to his wrist, shattering it instantly. He retaliated with a carapace covered foot to my chest, sending me across the room. Bullets and plasma bolts continued to fly through the air. One of the crabs had been strung up by Lenny, pinned to the ceiling, another was bleeding out on the ground, a gaping hole in his stomach, and the one I'd disarmed was fumbling for his pistol. One of Lenny's arms quickly flung it across the floor to my feet.

The bolt left the barrel at an incomprehensible speed, the heat from the matter conversion searing my flesh and causing me to drop the gun. I heard the thump of the crab I'd disarmed as he dropped to his knees. His head was gone, only a smoking stump left where his neck had been. All guns suddenly turned to the single guard still standing.

"Surrender," Magpie stated in a grim tone, "Or you'll wish she had gotten you with that one."

"Fine," She growled, her voice being the first thing that had indicated her gender, "You win. What do you want? Info?"

"On your knees," Magpie began to approach her, "Don't make me repeat myself." The chitinous mercenary slowly lowered herself to the ground, careful not to move too suddenly.

"What do you want?"

"I didn't tell you that you could speak," Magpie smashed her across the side of the head with her gun, a loud crunch filling the room and leaving a visible crack in her head. She held the barrel up to her throat and forced her head back. "Now... Beg."

"I would never."

Magpie cocked the gun.

"... Please."

"Louder."

"Please! Don't kill me. This is just a job, I-"

"The day you let them turn you into a fucking lobster you lost any right to say this is just a job. People like you sicken me. So desperate for that thrill of exerting power over people that you sell yourselves into something most people choose death over. I've killed so many of you crabby bastards, dozens, maybe hundreds. Every single one of them deserved it. What makes you different?"

"I have a family, plea-"

"The last person who said that to me got to watch their house burn down before I put a glory hole in their skull. Come up with something original."

I was in awe, watching my sister echo the kinds of rants our father had gone on countless times before I left. I knew where it came from. An urge to protect. Me, the gang, everyone in this cesspit. That didn't change how much it frightened me. I didn't see the little girl I'd stuck up for as a child, I saw the ghost of my father, as full of righteous fury as when he was alive. Then I saw a flash, and I heard my sister yelp in pain.

I could see the light from outside coming through the hole in her torso. Her legs fell out from under her. There was a stunned silence. The cancer guard on her knees looked as confused as anyone else, at least as much as her rigid features would allow.

"Run," a weak voice sputtered, "Get out of here, Captain." The guard on the ground, a gaping wound in his gut to match Magpie's, cried out desperately. In the panic, the captain fled, some of the gang members tailing her. Lenny's hands burst from the floorboards and wrapped around the head of the guard on the floor, snapping his neck so violently he was nearly decapitated. I dragged myself to Magpie's side.

"Mel, Mel, Can you hear me?" I held her clawed hand.

"It's… Cold. Sis…"

"I'm here Mel, it's okay, I'm right here."

"Don't let go, please, I don't want to go… Not yet…"

"You won't, it's okay, I won't let you go."

A thick globule of blood and mucus flew from her beak as she sputtered. Her intestines were visible through the gaping tunnel through her body. One of Lenny's hands clutched my shoulder, I turned to see this one was connected to a body.

"It's fine, I've got her," he nodded, other arms coming in from all sides to carefully sterilize the wound and staunch the bleeding. "It's lucky it was a plasma bolt, the heat already did a lot of the work for me. I've made some calls, someone'll be here for her, I can keep her stable until then."

"You're sure?"

"I'm sure," His poker face needed work. I didn't let go of my sister's hand.

"You hear that, Mel? You're gonna be fine."

"Yeah," she coughed, "I have so much faith in a butcher's ability to keep me alive."

"In all fairness, the meat I work with *is* still alive."

"Touché," she laughed faintly but it quickly devolved into a retching cough.

Chapter Eight: Questions

Cold wood caressed me uncomfortably, like bony arms desperately searching for warmth. A knot of anxiety and rage twisted in my stomach like a snake trying so hard to be born, the promise of fresh meat just inches away, arms bound and a bag over its head. The crab opposite me began to rouse, one of his legs irrevocably shattered from where Lenny had pinned him to the ceiling. I held my hedgehog, its quills rustling with anticipation. A smartly dressed merwoman pulled the sack from his head, a piranha-toothed snarl clear through the transparent skin of her waterbrace.

"Awake?" She traced a taloned hand along his carapace, leaving distinct scratches in the black, glossy surface. He only groaned in response.

"I've got it from here," I gestured to the door with my head.

"Alright, but if he gives you any guff I'll be right outside," She nodded. The heavy door closed slowly behind her, a distinct click resounding as it shut.

"You got a name?" I leaned back uncomfortably in the chair.

"Misha," He stated plainly.

"Well Misha, you should consider yourself lucky. Y'see, if I had been the one hollowed out by that blast, you'd be staring down Magpie right now. Lucky you, you've got me."

"Ah, so you're the good cop then?" His words came with a thick but indistinct accent, not uncommon. He was likely second generation, raised in the slums in a communal home.

Not hard to imagine why he'd choose this over that stigma and powerlessness.

"No," I shook my head, "No, but I'm giving you the courtesy of saving enhanced interrogation until *after* you resist." I imagined what Magpie would have done by now. Gouged his eyes out, tore a limb from its socket, salted the wounds. That's what Dad would have done if he were in this chair, and my sister, the dutiful shadow she is, would have done likewise.

"May as well get to torture then, I won't talk."

"I think you will."

"What makes you so sure?"

I raised the hedgehog to his face, "If you don't give me anything useful, quills start flying."

"Bah," he shrugged in his seat, "Your little peashooter can't pierce my hide."

"No," I unfurled a surgeon's tool kit, along with a few items more at home with a carpenter, "That's why every time you refuse to answer, I get to shuck you like an oyster."

He remained silent, giving me a chance to get a good look at the creature he'd sacrificed his flesh to. It's true that cancer guards were, biologically, not much different from victims of the crustacean plague. In fact, they were its progenitors. Early field tests had proven less sterile than they seemed, the parasites that formed their armours managing to spawn in the wild, free to infect unwilling hosts. The figure before me, however, bared little resemblance to the likes of Frankie. His parasitic armour was a newer model, conforming more closely to the human form it had consumed. Frankie had gone from a jolly old man who conjured images of christmas to a crustacean beast, much sharper and bulkier than any human should be. The man before me looked as though he could have been wearing a suit of amour, smooth and black, conformed tightly to the slim figure that he presumably had before succumbing to the crustacean. The head was the giveaway. The eyes looked a little too wet, the modified gills that filtered the toxic air may have resembled standard respirators, but they expanded and contracted with each breath. The carapace could nearly pass for a helmet, but it was too small, too tight, and I felt suddenly curious about how much bone it had eaten through to get that way.

"Where did your captain go?"

"How should I know?"

"Do you have a base, a rendezvous point, anything?"

"We do, but she's alone now, she has no reason to go there. She won't expect any of us to come back alive."

"Where is Xander Maxwell?" Misha remained silent. I grabbed a screwdriver from the toolkit.

"Maxwell… I cannot say, it violates the terms of our contract."

I stood up, lifting his broken leg onto a small stool. "I'm not big on contracts." I plunged the screwdriver's flat end into the joint of the knee, working carefully around it to sever the membranes that held it in place. He howled with pain and the steel slid under the kneecap, the pitch and volume raising as I levered it from his body with a sickening wet crunch.

"Please," he sobbed, "I'll tell you anything…"

"Maxwell. Where is he."

"On the move, he was headed here. The captain will have met him by now. They know where you're heading, they'll cut you off, and they won't be alone."

"Atta boy," I smiled, burying the screwdriver in his shoulder. He cried out. I opened the door. "Kate," the blue scaled girl's face was plastered with an ear to ear grin, rows of needle teeth exposing themselves, I pointed to the weeping crustacean, "Lunch time."

Chapter Nine: Catching Up

"Frankie's budget biotech, Frankie speaking."

"It's Tiff, can you put Beth on?"

"Oh, one sec," A door creaked open in the background and I heard Frankie shuffling down a flight of stairs, "It's for you."

"Tiff?" Bethany's voice crackled through the speaker, "Is everything okay?" Her voice came with an awkward static, filtered through two degrees of separation.

"I wouldn't say okay. Things have been kind of... You know."

"What's the matter?"

"I had to go through the slums to avoid Maxwell, and everything's been going south since. Dad's dead, Mel got shot, and Maxwell knows where I'm headed."

"Oh god, babe, I'm sorry."

"It's fine, really, I- I'm gonna kill him. I'm gonna kill that bastard, I promise. He sicked some crabs on us, they made the mistake of putting a hole in my sister. Now he's made an enemy of half the slums. I just... I wanted to hear your voice again, in case-"

"No."

"What?"

"No, no in case. You're going to make it through this. I believe in you. When you see Maxwell, you put a quill between his eyes for me, him and anyone who gets in your way. You didn't get this far just to have a lowlife like him stop you."

"Babe..."

"Yeah?"

"I love you."

"I love you too." There was a long pause, for a moment I felt like I could take on the world, even when I was faced with the crushing reality that I would probably have to do exactly that. I swallowed the knot in my throat, not wanting to dwell on the task ahead.

"How have you been keeping? Frankie treating you alright?"

"He's a sweetheart, I'm doing great. Well, aside from the obvious."

"Claude's not that bad," I laughed.

"They are!" She protested. "I swear, they never stop talking! I pretend to be asleep just to shut them up but it takes them a good half hour to notice. I can't believe you ever-"

"Babe."

"No, seriously, what did you-"

"Babe!" I chuckled down the receiver, "You're starting to sound jealous."

"I just don't get it," she laughed.

"They're funny!"

"They're obnoxious! I just had to listen to them talk for a solid three hours about how they got arrested smuggling bioweapons, *swallowed one of the embryos*, and then regurgitated it in their cell, incubated it and used it to escape."

"That sounds like a fun story!"

"It sounds like a fun story when I summarize it in a sentence, it took them *three hours* to tell that."

"How did you get them to stop?"

"I told them they should write a memoir, they've been typing away on an old desktop for the last hour."

"Okay, I'll admit, I'm going to keep that in mind the next time I talk to them." We started laughing, it felt like the weight of the world fell off my shoulders for that moment. The laughter faded into a content silence. It was Beth who chose to break it.

"Promise me something?"

"Anything."

"When this is all over, when you drop off your cargo and get the money, when I get a new body… Take me to the carnival."

"That's all?"

"All?" She sighed, she sounded like she was smiling, even if it was only a rusted speaker grill producing her words, "That would mean the world to me."

Chapter Ten: Call to Arms

The supply room that had been used for the interrogation looked like a crime scene, and I suppose it was. Blue, copper rich blood splattered the walls and dripped from Kate's piranha teeth. She lay in the centre of the massacre, half asleep and surrounded by cobalt viscera. Misha's legs were still placed firmly on the chair, but everything from the waist up and been hollowed out and scattered around the room, desiccated husks of the cancer guard. Kate held his arm to her chest and sucked the cerulean drippings as she gnawed on the shoulder. I kicked her lightly on the shoulder to rouse her from her post-feast daze.

"Whaddyawant," she slurred, before her black eyes snapped to focus. "Oh, sorry, I um… I didn't recognize you for a second." She pulled herself awkwardly to her feet, clutching her engorged stomach and wiping the blood from her mouth. She slid her waterbrace back over her mouth and gills, relishing the more comfortable and passive method of respiration.

"Get ready, we're going." I scowled, trying to maintain an air of seriousness.

"Going?"

"He spilled the beans before you picked him clean, the captain is meeting with Maxwell and they're planning to cut me off on my way to make this delivery. We're gonna get him back for what he did to Magpie."

"Oh, sure, just um… Give me a minute to clean up," she scampered off down the hall. I examined the remnants of

Misha. She'd really done a number on him, even just from the head that was clear. Her claw marks were still preserved, four clear gouges along the right cheek. The head was completely hollowed out, the entire cavity visible through the empty eyes. There was no bone, not even a faint trace of it. Not in the skull, not in the arms, not in the chest. The parasite must have eaten it all, the only thing left of the host was the brain and the nerves, and all of that was in the stomach of a fish. I wondered if this was what Frankie looked like, on the inside. His parasite was older, wild, it had been divorced from the sleek, lab grown counterparts by generations. If you looked at them side by side, you wouldn't even recognize them as the same species. The cancer guard were pristine, almost mechanical in appearance. Every aspect of the crustacean plague was organic, and it did nothing to hide that.

    I followed Kate's route after a time, eventually making my way to what would be called the foyer in a fancier building, here it was just the hub. Magpie's gang was gathered, littered with faces both new and familiar. Some I knew as children, now grown and weathered by the cruelty of the slums, others had been adults during my time here, and their faces seemed to wear the same stoic looks eroded into them by years, though fresh scars and greying hair made them appear so much older. I stood at the front of the room, a small platform, barely a step really, served as a stage. The eyes of hundreds of hardened criminals fell on me, and I felt strangely at home.

    "I trust you all know why we're here. Your leader, my sister, has been shot. She's in critical condition. The man responsible is Xander Maxwell." The crowd booed and hissed at his name. "And we're going to fucking kill him." The booing turned to cheers. I saw Kate stumble into the back of the crowd.

It didn't take much after that to corral the gangsters into their vehicles, I stared out at them, tinged red by the lenses of my respirator. The handlebars of my bike were cold in my hands, and as I took the lead of the horde I couldn't help but think that my father would be proud. We continued along the same route I had planned, and I was thankful that Maxwell was such a despicable bastard. If he wasn't it might have been hard to gather up my own personal angry mob. We moved for hours, leaving the slums and finding ourselves in the barren wasteland that lay beyond them, a place where only monsters and madmen dwelled. A place I'd made more than my fair share of deliveries to. The wastes were lawless, unregulated, and sterile. Just dust and sand, and the things that refused to die off. My bike ground to a halt, the swarm of vehicles behind me following suit.

"Holy shit," I heard Kate's voice from the car directly behind me.

I stared out into the distance, hundreds of crabs, Maxwell's goons, beasts the size of tanks mounted with an arsenal that could take out a small nation. All the backup money could buy. I could only think of one thing as I looked out at the horde.

"We're all going to die."

Chapter Eleven: Collision

Maxwell stood at the front of his legion, flanked on either side by the goons from the motel. He stepped forward, and I did the same, our respective armies awaiting some signal. His furrowed brow told me that he was about as happy to see me as I was to see him.

"Nice vanishing act, still not sure how you pulled it off, but I'm guessing it's something to do with them?" He held the small card between his fingers, the red ink still emblazoned on it. "I called the number, but they weren't too chatty. I figure whatever you're carting around for them must be worth something if they're outfitting you with a personal teleporter. Maybe worth enough for me to forget about all of this and walk away."

"You're not getting it," I stood firm.

"Alright," he shook his head, "I'm sure you remember Bozo," he gestured to the grotesquely muscular beast of a man who stood gripping the mechanical hand grafted to his stump, "He definitely remembers you. And of course, Slit." He pointed to the thin, jagged man, all bones and spines. Another figure stepped out from behind him. Thin, covered in slick, black chitin. "And of course, Captain Alvarez." The crustacean hissed with rage as her eyes fixed on me.

"Murderer."

"Just so you know," I smirked, "Misha survived. Just long enough to rat you out and get eaten alive." Alvarez tried to lunge at me, but Slit put an arm out to stop her.

"She's goading you," He snarled, "Take another step and her men will tear you apart."

She looked to the small army of gangsters behind me, and her jaw split, unsheathing her chittering mouthparts and she screamed, "They can fucking try!" She knocked Slit's arm aside and lunged at me, but barely took two stops before the shot rang out. She dropped at my feet, motionless, and Maxwell's gun smoked.

"No one gets to kill her," He growled, "No one but me. Now, I'm gonna ask you one more time. Hand over whatever you're bringing the reconcilers, and I call off the crabs. No one else has to die today."

"You're wrong."

"I am?"

"You are. I made a promise. You're not walking away from this." I pulled my stun baton from its place and cracked it over Maxwell's wrist before he could react, the gun flying from his hand. Both sides made a charge, the ground shook with the force of hundreds of feet, the thunderous sound almost drawing my attention away from the lumbering brute taking a swing at me, my baton meeting his metallic hand and lighting him up like a christmas tree. Bozo dropped like a ton of bricks, forcing me to leap back. Slit charged, slashing at me with the bone spurs protruding from his hand like knives. Two of them got me in the arm, gouging out a deep chunk of flesh. He tackled me to the ground, his sharpened body digging into me as his comparatively soft palm wrapped around my neck.

"I'm gonna cut your fucking eyes out, you bitch," His bladed fingers loomed over the lenses of my respirator, poised to embed themselves in my skull. He reared back, ready to bring down his talons, when he suddenly went flying through the air. Kate's foot hovered over me, her pant leg shredded and her blood dripping on to me. She extended a scaly hand to help me back to my feet.

"Thanks, I was about two seconds away from being a shishkebab," I sighed.

"Anytime," Her smile was as flirtatious as it was sharp. A stampede of suited men, women and assorted others, all carrying enough firepower to take out an elephant, wrapped around us and charged onwards. Maxwell retreated into his crustacean swarm, equally armed to the teeth. The two fronts clashed explosively, bursts of plasma and the ringing of gunfire filled the air, the smell of ozone and charred flesh spreading across the arid battlefield. I saw the slithering mass of Lenny moving between the feet of the combatants, swallowing up crustaceans and pulling the injured from the front lines. One of his bodies materialized beside me, wrapping a bandage around the bloody gash in my arm before I could even fully register his presence.

"You ladies alright?"

"Yeah, Len, we're good."

"Great, great, sorry I can't stick around, need to shift my focus elsewhere," his body dissolved into fleshy tendrils and slipped away towards the point where the two forces collided. I unsheathed my hedgehog and began to limp forward, my leg more injured by the fall than I realized.

"Tiff," Kate put a webbed hand on my shoulder, "You don't need to go this, you're hurt, they can handle themselves."

"Sorry, I have to."

"No, you-"

"I made a promise," I shrugged her off, she was swallowed by the sea of suits as I trudged on. I got closer to the front line, which was progressively sliding backwards as more and more of the crabs fell. I could see their bodies littering the ground, crushed underfoot and mingled with my fallen allies. *There's no time for mourning*, I thought, gripping my hedgehog tight. It's quills were still, focused, it felt… Anxious. It knew what was coming. I saw one of the tank beasts on the horizon, the same unsettlingly human face as the Sweepers, contorted into a look of pain. This was a different pain, not the pain of living that the Sweepers experienced, this was the pain of dying. Lenny's mass converged on it, only barely covering it's back half, but still enough to crush its innards. Blood gushed from its body, and the crunch as it fell told me it had taken out a fair number of Maxwell's men with it. Another of the creatures reared up, showing disgustingly swollen human digits on the end of its bulky saurian forelimbs. The cannons on its back fired and it hit the ground, raining down explosives on Lenny, and a number of combatants from each side. A huge bony spur erupted from the ground at its feet, surviving portions of Lenny's mass merging together and puncturing the thing's brain with frightening speed, then worming inside the carcass to maneuver it like a marionette. He turned its ghastly bulk and artillery on its own side, blowing holes in the chitinous horde. From above it would have likely looked like a child was aimlessly burning ants with a magnifying glass, but from my vantage point there were only distant explosions and a faint blue mist that reeked of copper.

I pushed through the cold, hard bodies of the crustaceans, cracking their shells and exposing the meat inside with my baton. Even in the little wisps that permeated the whole battlefield, that was enough for Lenny to burrow inside them and scramble them like eggs. More than a few fists came from the mass of shell and flesh that surrounded me, but a few bruises were nothing to me with the adrenaline in my blood and the serpentine knot of rage in my stomach. I heard it hissing, calling out for blood, and it had its eyes set on one man. One man who I could feel myself getting closer and closer to.

"Maxwell!" I howled at him, he stood in the crowd of crabs, cowering behind them. I limped forward, Lenny forcing his bulk to surround me and push back the hordes. My hedgehog's eye focused on Maxwell, on the point right between his pupils. If it could breathe it would have been holding its breath.

"This is on you, Rose! All this bloodshed! All 'cause you don't know when to give up!"

"This," I choked on the foul air, only now realizing I had lost my respirator in the chaos. The red I saw now was my own blood seeping into my eyes. "This is for all the women you hurt, you bastard."

My hand shook as I prepared to pull the trigger, and then the world went sideways. I hit the ground hard, feeling the blood pool around my head. Bozo loomed over me, a satisfied grin on his face, his skin charred in parts. "That was for my hand," He leaned over me, "And this is for that stunt with the baton." He drove me a kick to the gut and I was thankful that his legs weren't as monstrously overdeveloped as his torso, even as I involuntarily spat a mouthful of blood.

"Take her carrier," Maxwell commanded, "Let's see what all this was for." The lumbering giant ripped the carrier from my back and I felt my arm dislocate as he yanked the strap out from under me. Slit walked up beside him, eager to examine its contents. He rifled around in the carrier, then pulled out the cylinder in his meaty grip. Maxwell's eyes went wide with shock. "A brain tube? All this shit for a stinkin' brain tube! Slit!" He took a breathe, then said, calm as you like, "Cut her fucking throat."

"It would be an honour," The jagged silhouette loomed over me, nothing but knives in the harsh sunlight.

"Boss," Bozo's inhumanly deep voice came, "I... I don't think this is a brain." The next few seconds were a blur of light and noise. Bozo screamed, and then Slit followed suit, then the world went yellow.

I was on my feet, still beaten and bruised, but no broken bones and not bleeding out. The cylinder stood upright at my feet, still glowing faintly with a yellow light. The crustaceans had backed away in terror, at least the ones who hadn't been reduced to scorch marks in the now crystalized sand. Maxwell was screaming, fear and rage mixing together in an incomprehensible string of obscenities, and then I saw what he was looking at.

Bozo. Bozo and Slit. Bits of them, at least. It had both of their faces, and they were both screaming in agony. Bozo's prosthetic had melted, the skin around it scorched and steaming. Slit's hand pawed uselessly at his neck, carving away bloody chunks but failing to bleed himself out. There was no artery to find there, not anymore. The main body was just spikes and muscle, flexing and heaving uncomfortably, piercing itself with every involuntary spasm.

"Holy shit," I stared at the canister at my feet. "What the fuck have I been carrying?" I asked no one in particular.

"You-" Maxwell's gaze snapped to me, "You... You're fucking dead, you hear me, de-" The quill landed right between his eyes. He dropped to his knees. I had never seen someone die by a hedgehog before, I'd heard the stories. They mutate the cells, causing overproduction. The original idea was to make a discreet weapon that gave the victim an aggressive cancer. The reality was anything but discreet. The victims of a hedgehog's venom ballooned, their body being overcome by tumours. Organs often ruptured the skin, though in most cases, the cause of death was suffocation. Xander Maxwell, within under a minute of being pierced by the quill, didn't look much different from Bozo and Slit. A formless, twitching pile of flesh, but there wasn't enough of Maxwell left to scream.

The cancer guard looked on in horror, glancing nervously at one another. The gangsters had fallen silent after the burst of yellow light consumed the battlefield. I looked around, the fallen bodies of Maxwell and his lieutenants as good as dead at my feet.

"The scumbag who signs your paychecks is a tumour, there's nothing left for you to fight over. Go home." They looked around, some falling back immediately, others still staring at the crystalized ground, and the blackened shadows of their fallen comrades. "Did I fucking stutter? Go home!"

And just like that, the crabs, their flesh tanks, everyone was gone but the dead and dying. I looked out to my ragtag army, standing on a sea of glass, then to the cargo I'd been charged with. I lay the thing back in its carrier, whispering under my breath, "What have I gotten myself into," and turned to the ones who'd followed me into hell and made it out alive. "I can make it the rest of the way alone. Thank you, for everything."

Kate stepped forward, hat in her hands, "It was an honour to meet you, Ms Magpie. I'd heard stories but… You're really something else."

"It's Rose." I laughed, "I haven't been a Magpie in a long time."

"Rose… It suits you," She put a hand on my cheek. I swept it away.

"Be careful of the thorns."

Chapter Twelve: Journey

Hours passed, images of the twitching husks of Maxwell and his cronies still burned into my mind. The yellow glow of the canister still lingered in the corners of my vision, a single question crossed my mind, and it dredged up memories of the red text scrawled on the card.

"**IN CASE OF EMERGENCIES ONLY.**"

I recalled the anguish on the faces in the mound, their self mutilation in pursuit of a death just out of reach. I couldn't escape their horrible mewling cries, or the shadows of the crustaceans etched into the glass where there had been desert. *If anything constitutes an emergency,* I reasoned, *this was it.* I slid my phone into its clip on my respirator, still intact even after being recovered from the battlefield, dialling in the crimson digits. The voice that answered was a weak rasp, barely audible over the sounds of my bike and the rushing wind.

"Ms Rose," it began, a dower monotone that seemed less than thrilled to hear from me, "I'm glad to hear from you. We were becoming worried after the news reached us about your… Confrontation."

"What the fuck am I carrying?" I cut through the niceties, or at least tried to.

"All in good time, Ms Rose. I trust Maxwell won't be bothering us again? You really should be more careful with your cards. You may develop a… Reputation."

"Is that a threat?"

"Heavens no," he wheezed in mock politeness, "Merely some friendly advice."

"What. Am. I. Carrying."

"Something very special, and very valuable. I'm afraid I'm not at liberty to say any more."

"Tell me, or so help me God I will turn this cycle around and sell this thing to the highest bidder."

"Now, now, Ms Rose. If you're unhappy with our arrangement, I am happy to renegotiate." *Reconcilers*, I had to fight not to spit when their name crossed my mind, *Nothing but money to burn*.

"I want answers."

"We'll double your fee," a pause came after he spoke, a silent contemplation.

"Two hundred and fifty percent," I stated flatly, "Or I walk."

"You are quite the haggler, Ms Rose. You have a deal." The phone clicked, and his voice disappeared. I was happy to not have his rasp in my ear. I checked the crude nav display wired into the handlebars of my bike. The abstract green lines painted a vague image of the geography in the area, a small counter giving a rough idea of how much farther to my destination. Less than two days, if I didn't stop moving. I felt on some level that maybe it would be achievable, but the sting of a sharp inhale told me otherwise. Whatever terrible thing was in that canister had knitted me back together, bathed in its amber glow. I hadn't realized how bad a state I was still in, the revival coming with a sudden burst of vitality. That had begun to wear away, and staring into the cloud-swallowed sky, faint trickles of midday sun coming through in little beams, the exhaustion was hitting me all at once. Every breath burned, even if my lungs weren't punctured, they were certainly still bruised.

I moved to unclip the phone, tempted to use it to find the coordinates for the nearest motel, but something else crossed my mind. A glimmer of concern. Lenny had given me the number before I rode on, once he'd reconstituted himself from the flesh of the tank beasts. My fingers worked along the small keypad and the phone buzzed, anticipating an answer.

"Tiff," The voice came, laboured as my own was sure to sound.

"I didn't wake you, did I?"

"No, no, I've been up for a while," Magpie croaked, "Lenny told me… Everything. What have you gotten yourself into, sis?"

"I wish I knew. Maxwell won't be pestering me anymore, him or the crabs. All that's left now is to meet the Reconcilers and get this thing off my hands."

"Oh god," She groaned, "You didn't tell me you were working with those Divine Reconciliation nuts. They're worse than Maxwell!"

"Their money's good."

"I have money, if you need help, why didn't you just come to me?"

"We weren't exactly on the best of terms."

Her silence spoke volumes.

"They offered me more than double, and they were already paying a lot."

"You're carrying a bio WMD, Tiff!" She cried out, "That thing is a nuke with a heartbeat, it's dangerous!"

"It's saved my life twice now."

"Don't tell me you're getting attached to that... Thing!"

"I'm not, I'm eager to be rid of it but... It's more than just a weapon. I need to find out what it really is."

"Tiff..."

"Melanie."

"Don't do anything stupid."

"Wouldn't dream of it."

Chapter Thirteen: The City of Snakes

The night came, and the moon seemed so much brighter than the sun through dusk's lighter smog. It illuminated my next stop, almost mistakable for a metropolis in the lunar luminescence. I slowed my bike to a halt as a trader passed, just another wanderer in the night. She wore a headscarf that obscured most of her features, but I could tell by the little I could see, the faint yellow gleam of her eyes and how they blinked along the wrong axis, the thickness of her skin, and most blatantly by the creatures that she travelled with, that she was a Serpentine. She was perched on the back of a creature that could have been mistaken for an unmodified alligator if it were sitting, but standing it was clear that its legs were long, horselike, built for sprinting. Another creature hopped in tow, tethered to the mount by its neck. It strongly resembled a frog or a toad, fat and bulbous with a wide and dripping mouth, bulging eyes utterly unfocused, almost blind with cataracts that showed its age. Large, open sores lined its back, or at least things that resembled sores. The reality was almost more sickening.

"Care to trade?" The woman spoke, eyes locked on mine.

"You got anything to drink?"

"Water? Or perhaps something... Else?" She could tell I was an outsider, my scaleless skin made it abundantly obvious. No Serpentine would ever make such an obvious allusion to the sale of alcohol to another of their kind. Their faith strictly forbade intoxication, the sale or consumption of illicit beverages carrying penalties ranging from fines to execution depending on the particular settlement.

"Water," I nodded, "Water'll be fine."

"Certainly," She dismounted, approaching her amphibious follower. She rolled up her sleeves before pausing, "You have cash, yes?" I pulled my wallet out and held it aloft, the Serpentine nodding and returning her focus to the creature before her. She knelt down and buried her arm in one of the puckered, oozing holes in its back, sinking in up to the elbow and rummaging around a moment. She pulled her hand free, the sudden release of the suction almost sending her tumbling into the sand. She held a glistening bottle of ice cold water, sealed and surprisingly clean. "That will be three Boros," she smiled, the covering on her mouth having slipped down to reveal a lipless, fanged grin. She looked at me after a second of counting my money, then laughed, "Apologies, seven credits." Seven credits was an outrageous price for water, even in the desert, but haggling was a custom of the serpentine. I lacked the energy, and the knowledge that my money troubles would soon be nothing but a memory had me feeling generous. I handed her a ten.

"Keep the change," I smiled, removing my respirator long enough to take a drink. Her eyes lit up as she stuffed the note into her flowing garment, as if she was worried I'd change my mind if she wasn't quick enough.

"Thank you," She gave a slight bow as she stepped backwards to her reptilian steed, "May the devourer smile upon you."

"And upon your clutch," I recited unthinkingly, an almost instinctual response drilled in during my rudimentary education. I had been expected to learn a few common greetings of the cults in the wastes, my father being slightly more accepting than most slum dwellers and just about anyone in the cities, at least enough to trade with them. I retained a fair number of connections across the wastes, making it easier to find work. The young Serpentine seemed a little taken aback at an outsider responding as I had, but smiled again and was shortly on her way again, vanishing into the sandy expanse with her toad in tow.

  I pressed on, thankful for the rehydration but still in need of a place to sleep. I regretted not asking the girl if she knew a place. Sand turned to cobbled paths as I crossed the border to the settlement. It wasn't unique by the standards of the Serpentine, who in turn were not unique by the peculiarities of the wastes. They shunned most inorganic technology, opting to use organic alternatives wherever possible. Their streetlights were grown rather than built, little larvae planted like seeds that rooted in place and grew upwards, a long exoskeletal shell terminating in a brilliant bioluminescent bulb. The people of the settlement rode on similar galloping reptilian things to the young trader, some even walking the hatchlings on leashes like housepets. Like most Serpentine settlements, the night was the more active time. The wastes are rife with predators, but most are courteous enough to hunt in the day time, the ones who did hunt at night relying on body heat, something the Serpentine lacked.

  Most of the inhabitants avoided eye contact with me, or shielded the eyes of their children. My bike, my respirator, even the small implant in my neck all marked me as an outsider, and worse: A technist heathen. They wouldn't say anything, I could count on that. The Serpentine shunned technology for religious reasons, and had fled to the wastes to avoid it, but they understood that others walked their own path. I wouldn't be reprimanded, though I was likely to be in their prayers.

It didn't take too long to be beckoned in by a round little man, lipless scaly face contorted into a smile that radiated a kindness in spite of the venomous fangs it revealed. His voice carried the same soft roundness as his body, curved by a slight lisping hiss.

"You are an outsider, yes? A traveller? Looking for a warm bed?" His voice rose sharply to punctuate each break between statements.

"Yeah, you got one?"

"Yes, right inside," He gestured to the large clay and stone building behind him. This was still the outskirts of the settlement, buildings closer to the centre stretched high into the sky, massive organisms unto themselves that collected the trickles of sunlight and condensed them into fruit that sustained the Serpentines almost exclusively. The small man wandered into the building, gesturing for me to follow. The inside was a single open space, beds arranged along the circular walls of the room surrounding the elegant spiral staircase that led to higher levels. The man settled into the seat behind a little counter opposite the door, another door behind him leading to what I could only assume was either a staff room or his private bedchamber.

"It is twelve credits a night," he hissed cheerfully, "I assume you carry credits, you don't look like the type to deal in Boros. How long will you be staying."

"Just the night."

"Fantastic." He smiled as I slid the notes across to him. "I'll show you to your bed." He huffed and puffed as he trotted up the spiral staircase, taking me up two floors before finally leading me out to a room that didn't seem any different from the others. "Ha, it gets harder and harder to get up these in my old age. The sooner my son takes over the better," He laughed unsubtle about his annoyance.

"Family business?" I felt the need to ask.

"I hope so. I built this place with my own two hands. I want to keep it in the family when I return to the devourer but my son... He's not so keen on it, fancies himself a poet, wants to travel, find his muse. He doesn't want to be tied down to some musty old hostel." There was a long silence, the owner eventually snapping back to focus. "I apologize, you didn't come all this way to listen to an old snake's sorrows. Your bed," he gestured to the small rectangle of foam, covered in thin sheets, more of a mattress than a bed, "If you need anything I will be downstairs."

"Thank you," I nodded, watching as he vanished slowly down the spiralling steps. I threw my jacket and boots to the side of the small mattress, laying my respirator on top of them and my carrier to the side. My weight sank into the soft material with little resistance, the hardness of the floor apparent underneath. I stared into the ceiling, tracing its various cracks and imperfections. The old man hadn't exaggerated about building the place with his own two hands.

The sound of little feet disturbed my thoughts and drew my focus from the ceiling.

"Well hey, kiddo," I looked at the child standing over me, unmodified but wearing the garb of the Serpentine. A convert, or the child of converts at least. "You okay?"

"Are you gonna be a snake too?" She looked at me curiously.

"No," I laughed, "No, I'm just passing through."

"Good," she nodded, "My mommy used to look pretty like you, then she took me here and turned into a snake."

I blushed a little, and fought the urge to snicker at the kid's insinuation. "You don't think she's pretty anymore?"

"No," the child radiated a strange seriousness, "She used to have really pretty hair. Now she's all green and weird." Part of me wanted to scold the kid, but she wasn't mine to teach.

"I'm sure your mom is still pretty," I nodded, "Just different."

"I don't want my hair to go away!" She segued suddenly enough to cause whiplash, and I looked around, a little relieved there was no one around for her to wake up.

"It doesn't have to," I laughed, the little girl remaining stoic.

"Mommy says I'm gonna be a snake too, when I'm bigger."

"Do you know why she says 'when you're bigger?'"

"No..."

"There's a rule, you have to be big enough to make up your own mind." I remembered it from my studies. Most Serpentine were born into it, and born with the modifications as a result. There was a strict rule against the total conversion of children, it helped that growing bodies didn't take as well to gene mods.

"Really?"

"Yeah. When you're bigger, it'll be up to you what you want to do."

Another set of footsteps came, louder and heavier than the girl's. I saw her mother descending the staircase from the next floor up.

"Samantha!" She hissed, "What did I tell you about bothering people!"

"Sorry, Mommy."

"I'm so sorry about her," the mother apologized profusely, "She's having a lot of trouble adjusting, especially with, you know." She gestured to her face.

"It's alright, really, you have a lovely kid," I looked down to the girl, "Samantha, huh? I guess you were lying to me."

"No, I didn't!"

"Yes, you did," I laughed, "Your mother looks lovely." Samantha's mother snorted.

"Sam, please tell me you haven't been telling people I'm ugly."

"Sorry, mommy."

"Again, I am so sorry about her."

"Really, it's alright." And with that, the two returned to their floor and I returned to staring at the ceiling until I finally managed to fade out of consciousness.

Chapter Fourteen: Corpse Orchard

The spiral stairs creaked as I made my way down, the hostel owner snoozing in a small chair behind his desk. I was met with a shocking brightness as I crossed the threshold back into the Serpentine settlement. The smog was thinner in the wastes than in the city, but around the settlement it seemed almost non-existent. The hot midday sun was a rare sight, one I couldn't appreciate as its light left everything washed out and white. The settlement was utterly dead, not a soul in sight. A few of the reptilian steed lounged in small hides, two of the amphibious things that accompanied traders sat half submerged in baths of water, keeping their skin moist. The holes on their backs seemed to gape as they bobbed up and down, and I wondered if their pouches helped them store enough water to survive the long journeys across the desert. I mounted my cycle, avoiding moving at high speeds as I had no reason to stir the Serpentine during this hour.

    I moved steadily towards the centre of their settlement, to the great living structures that lay at its heart. I had learned a little in my youth about the culture of the Serpentine, enough to know that they didn't like the term outsiders gave these places. "Corpse Orchards," usually said with a look of disgust. Their true name was disputed, the Serpentine were after all a secretive group who didn't share such information readily with outsiders. I had once heard my father call them the devourer's gardens. The name made sense, though only as much as the less acceptable one. These were the burial grounds of the Serpentine, but they were never considered a place of death.

"The Serpentine don't believe in death," my father had once explained to me, "Not in the way we do. They believe in… Change." That was his way of explaining it. His knowledge came from a close relationship with Serpentine bootleggers, of course, so it was hard to say it was reliable. They told him how their dead, or rather their dying, were buried in the gardens, along with a little grub. The grub would burrow into the body, consuming it from within, and eventually it would "bloom." I had always imagined this as massive insects, bursting from the ground but still rooted to the spot. Now, driving through, I could see why the Serpentine saw this as a rebirth. A vast grove of beautiful, glimmering trees of obsidian, branching out with small orange growths, clear and shaped like perfect teardrops. These were the fruit of the so-called "Corpse Orchards." The trees grew taller and thicker towards the centre, never giving away their true nature as modified insects. The older trees had distinct pits in their surface, little tunnels that grew through the flesh. Approaching the largest, these tunnels were more defined, deeper and wider, eventually large enough for an adult to travel through. At the centre, the rooted monument to the founder. Each Serpentine settlement had one, but this was the most magnificent I'd seen. Homes had been built into its flesh, a whole town, not like the quaint little place on the outskirts, this was a metropolis carved into a living headstone.

    I didn't stay long, only enough to appreciate the majesty of it. Serpentine weren't fond of outsiders in their places of worship, let alone outsiders carrying sacreligious technology. The garden thinned out as I passed the founder's monument, eventually again meeting with the freshly laid graves of the serpentine, just beginning to bloom, and soon the settlement was another speck on the horizon, no different from the countless others.

    I felt the bristling quills of my hedgehog, pulling it out to take a closer look. "You okay, girl?" Its single eye rolled wildly, whipping back and forth between me and something to the east. "We're not going that way, we need to head south." It bristled louder, protesting in a way it never had before. I stopped the bike and looked to where its pupil was now fixed. I remembered this place. I'd come here a few years earlier, or at least somewhere near here. I suddenly understood what the hedgehog wanted.

    "You want to go home?"

Chapter Fifteen: Beneath the Sands

It was a ways out of the way but I knew that whatever was waiting for me at the drop point, I'd be better off with my best means of defense on my side.

"Alright, girl, just this once," its eyelids twisted oddly, in a look I decided was probably gratitude. It had been about five years since I last trekked out here. At the time I had never even heard of a hedgehog, but a client needed a pickup and this was the spot. I came to the heavy airlock of a bunker, more solid than anything I'd seen in the city by a wide margin. This was something built to last. A small intercom sat under a steel panel, and I pressed the little buzzer.

"Hello?" The voice was strangely warped in a way that was difficult to fully explain. Too deep, perhaps, or too resonant.

"I'm here to pick up a package for Mike Valentine, this the right place?"

"Ah, yes, one moment, I'll buzz you in." The airlock shuddered open, a decontamination shower later and I was descending an ancient staircase into the old workshop. A figure was hunched over a small workstation, dissecting a small, flabby thing that seemed to still be breathing.

"Um, hell-"

"It's over there," they cut me off, a long, bony arm extending from under their coat and pointing to the small organics case. Two other arms still worked away at the breathing, bleeding thing on the workstation. Tanks lined the walls, glowing green cylinders ranging from the size of test tubes to large enough to hold a person, bizarre fetal things floating inside them. "Are you still here? Go, take it and get out."

"Oh, I just-" The figure spun, and I met Doctor Chroma Stedman for the first time. It may have been a bit of an exaggeration to call them a doctor, to tell the truth. They considered themself a hobbyist, though it was clear they didn't do much else besides tinkering in their lab. Their face was shockingly normal, attractive even, which was a great contrast to the rest of their body. Six arms, all too long and too thin for a normal human but oddly fitting on Chroma's spindly form. Their chest was unnaturally long as a result, three sets of pectoral muscles sitting above their emaciated midriff. Long, dark hair was pulled back in a messy ponytail that trailed down their back.

"Close your mouth, you'll catch flies."

"I'm sorry, I just-"

"I really don't care, but I'm very busy as you can see, and unless you're a customer I'd rather get back to work." I glanced at the tanks of embryos that lined the walls, seemingly the only light source in the cramped den of mad science.

"What... Do you sell?" I wasn't sure I actually wanted to know. This was what finally caught Chroma's attention.

"You don't know?" I shook my head, "You came all this way... And you don't know?"

"Knowing isn't part of the job description."

"Ah, of course, a smuggler, I forgot. Most of my work is... Custom, but I do have a few specimens I keep around that may interest you. Are you familiar with... Hedgehogs?"

And like that, I bought her. She was only an embryo, Chroma provided enough nutrient solution to get her to maturity. I'd had a few more dealings with Chroma since, of course. I only ever spoke to them over the intercom in our subsequent encounters, and my hedgehog had never reacted like this. I reached the familiar bunker door and buzzed, awaiting a response. Silence. I buzzed again, and then a third time.

"What? What? What do you want?" The voice that came through was manic, but still recognizable as Chroma.

"No need to get so pressed, Doc it's just me."

"It's funny, I don't think that's an answer to what I asked."

"Well, I was just passing through and my hedgehog started acting up. Figured she wanted to check out her birthplace."

"What?"

"You know, come visit the old stomping grounds?"

"... It's a gun."

"Well, yeah, but-"

"Please tell me it hasn't started talking."

"What? No, it's like... Purring? Shivering? I don't really know how to describe it, but it seemed to react to the lab."

"Are you trying to suggest that your hedgehog has developed some level of sentience?"

"Don't they... All?"

Chroma paused, then sighed. "Come in, I need to figure out what's wrong." The airlock opened and I descended into the darkness of the lab. A thin layer of dust coated most of the surfaces, a number of tanks were shattered, green stains that retained the glow even after drying left in their places. There was no sign of Doctor Stedman.

"Doc? Doc? What do you mean by wrong?" Something rustled in a corner, instinctively, I withdrew the hedgehog from its place on my hip. "Doc..?" I stumbled through the darkness, toward the rustling. Something skittered along the floor, away from the corner. I kept the hedgehog outstretched, its eye following the sound. The quills closest to its tip stood erect, beginning to curl forward in preparation to fire. I pressed forward again, but turned on my heels as the sound suddenly came again from behind me. Nothing could be seen in the darkness of the lab. I took a step backward, eyes darting from wall to wall in the desperate hope that Chroma would emerge from the shadows and call me a triggerhappy fool, or whatever may be lurking in the dark would step out long enough to give me a clear shot.

"Doc?" I whispered, not wanting to rouse the attention of anything other than Chroma. A shadow crossed the wall, a small, sharp thing cast in silhouette against the green glow. My hedgehog fired without input, shattering a tank of the glowing liquid. A half-formed thing came tumbling to the ground with the shards of glass, fetal and mewling. As I stepped back something crossed under my foot, crunching as I tripped on it but scurrying onward regardless. I glared at the hedgehog in my hand, a look I could only describe as embarrassment in its single eye. I looked back to the embryonic thing, still crying in a puddle of blood and glowing green slime. It kicked and thrashed helplessly as something came from the shadows, limping towards it. Even in the green glow its form was difficult to decipher. Its back half was crushed almost flat, ruined legs dragging uselessly behind it. Its front didn't look much better, a pair of little grasping hands pulling it forward, inch by agonizing inch. Little spikes dotted its back, not unlike the quills of my hedgehog, but the worst of it was the face. Round, chubby cheeked with eyes swollen shut, a fat lipped mouth oozing saliva. It babbled in excitement as it sniffed the blood of the dying fetus, speeding up its crawl. As it moved closer there was no denying the thing's appearance. The face of an infant plastered onto a body that didn't really resemble anything, except maybe a biological waste bin. Its lips pulled back to reveal a mouthful of needle-like teeth, and it began to tear into the almost living, unborn thing, which screamed in agony before a sickening crunch silenced it. I watched on in terror as the spiny infant-thing gorged itself on its kin, then turned its hungry gaze onto me. I inched myself backwards, pointing the hedgehog in the creature's vague direction, but I never had a chance to fire. There was a flicker of motion, a thin, white strand descending from the ceiling for only an instant, and then it was gone, creature and all. I looked up, but there was nothing but darkness.

  The predator became prey; the infant-thing made a horrible sound, the sound you would expect a newborn to make while being eaten alive. The crunch of bones and sound of rending flesh was gut-churning, then all at once it stopped. The carcass hit the ground, shattering the few bones that had remained intact. Its underside was nothing but a bloody hole, exposing how it had been hollowed out. Then, the tail descended. It was long, several feet of exposed vertebrae, a bloodied blade at its tip. I surmised that this was the tool that had so swiftly penetrated the smaller beast, and I aimed my hedgehog at it, squeezing the trigger polyp several times in quick succession. Nothing. The hedgehog blinked a few times and its quills rustled, then receded into its fleshy barrel. "What the fuck, don't do this to me now," I whimpered, frantically pulling my stun baton out, illuminating the creature on the ceiling for a brief instant with the arcs of blue light as it telescoped from its handle. I made out more limbs than I could count, exposed bone, or an exoskeleton. The green and blue light did nothing to make its colours clear, but it was dark. Almost black. I held the baton out, as if the creature had a chance of understanding what the voltage would do to it. The tail receded, and there was a creak as the thing adjusted itself on the pipes it clung to. All at once, it dropped.

Fabric, patchwork fabric covered its massive frame. Its shape was almost impossible to determine under the covering, but from the trace of its underside I had seen I knew it was stick thin, the appearance of bulk created by its numerous splayed limbs. A long, clawed hand came out from under the white and brown tarp, and the creature padded forward. Its neck, just as terribly long and thin as the rest of it, pushed forward from the mass, like a turtle coming from its shell. Its shaggy mane shifted aside as it raised its head, exposing it to the faint green light.

"Hello, Rose," Chroma's face stared from the monstrous mass, wet with gore from the thing laying dead at their feet.

"Chroma? What the fuck? Are you okay?"

"Never better," They grinned, wiping the blood from their lips, "Apologies for startling you. One of my subjects escaped, I couldn't risk startling it. It's not as tame as your hedgehog, I'd be full of quills right now if I'd spoken."

"... You just wanted to fuck with me, didn't you?"

"A little bit."

"Dick! You absolute dick!"

"Temper, temper, Rose, not very ladylike."

"Oh fuck you, if anyone knows that gender roles are bullshit, it's you."

"Well said, care for a drink?"

"Not really, my breath still smells like apples from the last one I had."

"More for me," They chuckled. "Now, your hedgehog, mind if I take a look?" They stretched out a skeletal hand, almost insectoid in appearance. I placed the vertebral grip in their palm. They sniffed at it, the hedgehog barely reacting to their probing and prodding. It seemed to wince as they slid a razor sharp digit between the bones of its grip, tasting the bloody matter scraped from the joint. "Now that's interesting..."

"What, is she alright?"

"I need to take a sample, if that's alright." They didn't wait for a response before carving a small piece of flesh away, then running a finger along the base of her barrel, causing a quill to extend and detach effortlessly. "It seems like your hedgehog has an excess of neuroplastic, I'm not sure if that's genetic or environmental but my money would be on the latter. I only make one embryo per batch and just stimulate a separation before I put them on ice, so all its siblings are genetically identical. Have you had a high concentration of neuro-enhancers around?"

"Not that I'm aware of."

"Interesting. Anyway, I'll just dispose of this one and grow you a fresh-"

"No!"

"No?"

"I like her. You can't just kill her."

"You want to… Keep… The defective gun?"

"Yes."

"Alright, but when this inevitably comes back to bite you in the ass, don't come crying to me."

"Trust me, Doc, you are the last person I'd come to for sympathy."

"I'm glad."

Chapter Sixteen: Paradise Found

The land settled by the Church of the Divine Reconciliation was something else entirely to what I'd experienced on my excursions to the wastes. The barren desert where nothing thrived was swallowed up by grasslands. A vast meadow, which gave way quickly to tall and sturdy trees. Not like the insectoid things that grew in the devourer's gardens, these were honest to god leaf-and-wood trees. There was no sign of the people who called this place home, known for being a reclusive and strange lot. A creature, unlike anything I'd ever seen, fled from the roars of my bike. Brown and spindly, covered in soft fur with great, branching horns growing from its head. I stopped to watch the thing, but it vanished into the increasingly thick woodland before I had the opportunity.

"They used to call them deer," a voice came from behind me, "I suppose they still would if they existed elsewhere. This is the last place on earth to have any, and even then they're not perfect recreations." I turned to glance at the man, old and frog-eyed with a wide mouth and thin lips. His body was cloaked in robes, only his bald head poking out.

"Recreation?"

"I'm afraid so," he gave a grim nod, "They've been extinct in the wild for well over a century. We remade them from stored samples, but their respiratory system is… Heavily modified. It was that or outfit them all with respirators."

"But the trees, the air here is so clear."

"True, it isn't as harmful as the city air. A few hours would do no harm, but without the appropriate equipment I can't recommend breathing it for longer."

"So, the church has been… Planting trees?"

The old man cracked a smile, revealing a wide grin of perfectly flat teeth, herbivore teeth. It was the mouth of a prey animal. "We have been working to create something more… Sustainable. Trees are a part of that, and the deer, among others. Our own little pocket of Eden." The word was familiar, an extract from the half remembered ravings of a street preacher.

"I'm Tiffany Rose, I'm here to-"

"I know why you're here, Ms Rose, I was sent to escort you."

"Oh."

"If you would be so kind as to follow me," he uncrossed his arms, long, webbed digits stretching from the sleeves of his robe. His cheeks puffed, then his throat, adding to his frog-like appearance. A massive, fleshy growth swelled from his back, emerging from his robe, and his body began to rise into the air. His head deformed as the gas pocket continued to swell, becoming barely distinguishable from his torso. A burst of foul smelling air erupted from a vent on his back, his webbed hands working the air like paddles as he shot forward. I watched on in disgust and curiosity. "Come along," his voice had taken on a distinct baritone, far deeper than it had been just moments prior, "Wouldn't want to keep the high priest waiting!"

My cycle, even moving at top speed, could barely match the pace of this human airship as it weaved expertly through the treetops. He froze suddenly, coming to a more sudden stop than I thought would be possible for him. I ended up coming to a less elegant halt some distance ahead of him, narrowly avoiding the trunk of a tree.

"What is it?" I called up to him.

"Shh," he hissed, and I briefly wondered if he shushed me or if it was just escaping gases. A loud crash in the direction he was looking made me slightly more confident in my assumption that he had shushed me. I looked, but there was no sign of anything through the impenetrable veil of trees.

"Seriously, what's going on?"

"Shh," one of his flipper-like hands twisted to his mouth, the gesture telling me it was definitely a shush. Another crash followed, then another, then a tree came down just feet from me and left the great beast unobscured.

"So is this another one of your extinct creatures?" I backed up, drawing my hedgehog from its holster.

"No, no it most certainly is not," the old man's body swole to a greater extent and he floated higher until almost out of sight.

"Goddamned coward!" I yelled, taking another step back as the thing lumbered out of the shade the trees provided. Two colossal forelimbs crashed down in front of me, a pair of smaller ones connected behind them and scratching uncomfortably at the air. Its hindlimbs bent like a dog's, but ended in something akin to hooves. It had an almost human face, but too big, the neck swallowed by muscle. Four black eyes focused on me, the uncountable tendrils on its back writhing with glee. The stitches on its forehead were barely healed, still scabbed over and crusted with blood. Its mandible split down the middle, a long, tentacle-like tongue lolling out with trails of spittle and viscera clinging to it. In place of an opening at the back of its gaping maw was another set of jaws, smaller and more human. They worked awkwardly, wet and lipless, to form words in a familiar voice. The voice of Xander Maxwell.

"Miss me?"

Chapter Seventeen: The Great Beast

"Maxwell?!" I stumbled back, hedgehog trained on the seam between his eyes.

"In the flesh," he gestured to himself with his mid-limbs, "Like the new look?"

"I killed you, you son of a bitch!"

"You certainly tried." He wrapped his gargantuan fist around the fallen tree and swung it like a club, and I was instantly swallowed by yellow light. Suddenly I found myself behind him, the glow fading around me. My hedgehog unloaded quill after quill into his back, acting on instinct. "Still with the magic act?" He craned his muscular cone of a neck, "You need to pick up some new tricks." The quills left swelling welts on his back, but not nearly the explosive growth of flesh it had when he was still human.

"Fuck."

"You think I'd let them shove me into a new body without accounting for what you did to the last one?" He hurled the shattered trunk like a javelin and again the thing in the canister pulled me out of harm's way. The jumps in quick succession left me nauseated, and as I saw the swirling eye of my hedgehog I could tell that I wasn't the only one.

"So how'd you manage it?" I yelled, squeezing the fleshy trigger polyp and unloading more quills in Maxwell's direction, only hitting with two or three thanks to the hedgehog's disorientation.

"C'mon, you really think all those crabs were just gonna walk away when they were owed a debt?" He snarled, uprooting another tree.

"Figured they'd be a little put off by getting vaporized."

"Only meant a bigger bill." He reared back like a bull, ready to charge.

"So they did this to you? Some kind of special offer, hire out enough grotesque monsters and we'll turn you into one?" He barreled down on me, rising up to swing the mighty trunk with all his collected momentum. The crunch as it hit the trees that had been behind me was almost deafening, even as the yellow glow put some distance between us.

"This'd be over much faster if you just stayed still!" His neck snapped back in my direction without me so much as making a noise, and he dropped again to his four massive limbs, the middle two dangling aimlessly at his side. The posture was utterly beastly, there was so little human left in him, if there had ever been any to begin with.

"It's not like I'm doing this on purpose!" I yelled, unloading more rounds into his enormous body. The welts on his back were growing steadily, merging together into larger and larger tumours, swallowing up a number of the tendrils. A quill struck him in the eye and he recoiled, clutching at his face.

"Do you know how much this body cost me?" He howled, his hand dropping as he charged, revealing that the side of his face was already swelling greatly, swallowing up two of his empty, black eyes. "Damn Crabs left me a brain in a tank, fucking vultures, only needed enough to pay them. Getting this cost me a small fortune, all so I could rip you apart with my bare hands." His hands were only inches from my face, ready to make good on his promise, when the yellow light dragged me to safety. Maxwell crashed hard into the soft soil, partly burying himself. I doubled over, struggling to breathe. I felt the sluggishness of the thing in the canister, its golden glow growing dimmer with each jump.

"C'mon," I choked, "C'mon, you think you can take me? Try it!" I pulled the baton from my boot. Maxwell brushed mud from his swollen face, more growths becoming evident on his chest and arms.

"Not looking too hot, Tiff," He lurched forward slowly, savoring the moment, "How many more times do you think you can pull that stunt? Looks like it's really doing a number on you."

"Speak for yourself," I wheezed, "You look like you just lost a fight with a hornet's nest. How long can you tank those tumours?"

He smirked, or at least his inner jaw contorted in a way that read as a smirk. "I reckon I can last a little longer than you. That thing on your back, it's slowing down. Who's gonna give out first, you, me, or it?"

"Guess we'll just have to see." Maroon spikes loaded with carcinogenic venom flew, six in all, each and every one embedding itself in Maxwell's chest. He doubled over in pain and snarled.

"That wasn't very smart," his bulk rippled, more and more growths bursting from him with every second, "Not very smart at all." The tendrils from his back ballooned, then ruptured like zits, all the blood and gore giving way to bone tipped appendages, longer and thicker than the writhing things on his back. His shoulders swelled, as did his foremost and middle limbs, the bulk of his torso all but engulfing his head. The forelimbs tore and split as they grew, losing their form in favor of resembling the same writhing masses that erupted from his back. The middle limbs remained intact, though the divisions between the digits vanished as they swole together to form enormous club-like growths. The back end shriveled and withered, consumed as fuel for his horrific transformation.

"Woah, woah, this is… Not how this is supposed to go," I stepped back, then back again, then spun and broke into a sprint, no longer confident in my cargo to save me from the creature that had once been maxwell. It loomed high over the treetops now, casting a vast shadow across the wastes. It continued to grow, becoming increasingly amorphous as its body swole and ruptured in parts. The head had either completely vanished, been burnt up as fuel like the vestiges of legs, or was simply too small and distant to distinguish from the other ripping lesions that made up its formlessness. A piece of the thing crashed down in front of me, not distinct enough from the rest to truly be called a limb, just another portion of its mass. The great, whipping tendrils, all lined with bones and eyes, grabbed at the trees and the animals and even the grass, dragging it into the fleshy form to feed the growth.

"Well, I guess it's fitting," I yelled to the thing, not sure it could even hear, "You always were a blight Maxwell, it makes sense you'd be the one fucker who turns into a walking cancer after getting hit with this thing." The hedgehog looked apologetic, scared even, as I shoved it back into its holster. Even if she hadn't fired the last of her quills into Maxwell, meaning she'd need a few days to regenerate them, they obviously weren't going to do much good. A dim yellow aura swallowed me, not working fast enough anymore, I had to bat the groping tendril away with my baton. I vanished as it came back for a second strike, finding myself suddenly on the edge of the oasis.

"Okay, I guess desperate times," I reached into the carrier, leaving the sentence to hang. The dim glow of the canister illuminated the form of the thing inside. It had grown since I examined it in the motel, and here in the light of the wastes I could see it clearly through the viewport. Its body was soft, ovoid, numerous little legs twisting and writhing. A maggot, an enormous maggot, easily the size of a football. Its pale flesh was slightly translucent, the yellow light emanating from within it. As unpleasant that image was, the thing that was seared into my mind after the fact was its face. Human. Completely human. The face of a baby on the body of a maggot, and it looked on the verge of tears. "I… What are you?" Its eyes opened, and they gazed into mine. They were black, like little holes in the universe. Blacker than should have been possible, like they swallowed any light that crossed their gaze. "You… Can you hear me? God, I hope you can hear me. You've saved my ass on a couple occasions now, so I'm gonna take my chance and assume you like me, or at least think I'm useful, so please, please I am begging you. Help me." It blinked, twice, slowly. A yellow light streamed from it, and I held it fast in my grip. Suddenly, the world fell out from under me and my ears filled with the sound of rushing air.

"Oh god," I mouthed, unable to get the words out as I hurtled towards the ground. I was in the air, high in the air, the

Maxwell-beast turning its form up towards me. The front half opened, petals of meat and bone unfurling like a great, blooming flower. It had spread itself across the greenery, devouring it all, only stopping at its borders because there was simply nothing left to consume. I held the larval thing out in front of me, face turned to the ground, and I closed my eyes. Even through closed eyes, I was almost blinded by the all-consuming golden radiance. There was a screech, a buzzing, and then the overwhelming sound of silence. I felt something hook under my arm, then something else, and I braced myself to be swallowed by the behemoth below. The sound of rushing air ceased, and I came to a halt. I opened my eyes, still half blind from the light.

"Be not afraid," one of the forms silhouetted against the sky spoke in a deep and bellowing voice.

"You are saved," the other croaked. My vision began to recover, and looking down I saw the crater that had been a vast garden, and the great black scorch mark that had been Xander Maxwell. I tried to focus on the figures as I descended slowly to the earth. Frog eyed and bald headed, gas filled growths on their backs. The Reconcilers.

Chapter Eighteen: Ascension

"It's all gone..." I thought, a handful of ash slipping through my fingers. The oasis, the new world the reconcilers had been working toward. Gone. Scorched from the face of the earth in an instant. One of the reconcilers who brought me to the ground laid a hand on my shoulder consolingly.

"We created our Eden from nothing, and we can do it again. The damage caused here was nothing to what we've gained." His other long, fleshy hand stroked the canister containing the maggot child, and I instinctively pulled it away despite having less right to it than him.

"Your whole settlement is a nuclear shadow, this thing must be worth a lot to you if it makes up for the loss." I tried to keep the suspicion from my voice, but I felt it trailing across my face. The little frog-eyed man didn't seem to notice.

"Our settlement?" He chuckled, "No, Ms Rose, New Eden was not our settlement, simply a side project. Our Cathedral still stands, proud as ever."

"It... Does?" I looked around, nothing but levelled ground for miles around. The old man snorted, and raised a bony flipper to the sky.

"We do not spend much time on the ground, I'm afraid."

"Your Cathedral is... In the sky?"

"Why do you think we are as we are?" His throat bulged in demonstration. "We remade ourselves in the image of our great founder, Saint Gilbert, who gave unto us a new holy land beyond the clouds. There, by his grace, we have been free to work without fear of persecution."

"So how the hell am I meant to get up there? I can't exactly fly."

"We have arrangements in place for outsiders who wish to bask in His majesty." He raised his inhuman digits again to the sky, and following their path I saw it. Like a carriage, but there was no beast or motor on the front to pull it along. Four robed figures, swollen to the point of appearing spherical, all tethered by the feet to the box's corners. It touched down a few feet in front of me, the robed men deflating to the point of bobbing comfortably at the end of their tethers. The one who'd gestured to it hovered forward, opening a small hatch on its side. "Please," he bowed, "Ladies first."

The ascent was almost silent, the men above, if they were all men, made no noise as we rose through the air. Through the small portholes I could see the ashes below, and the city of the Serpentine on the horizon. Other settlements came into view as we travelled higher and higher, though each new one was harder to distinguish than the last, eventually appearing as little more than dark blotches on the white desert landscape.

"My name is Father Reynolds," the bloated little man opposite me broke the silence, "It is a pleasure to meet you."

"Likewise, padre."

"I would like to thank you for keeping our precious cargo safe on your journey. He is truly important to us."

"That so?"

"Yes! I have been asked not to say too much until you meet with the high priest but I am simply overjoyed, the day of Reconciliation is finally upon us! All thanks to you, Ms Rose!"

"It's just part of the job, really. Besides, the little guy's done more to save me than the other way around."

"Perhaps, but I'm sure you will be remembered by our people for eons to come! Saint Rose, the one who carried Him!" I did my best to hide my discomfort, but Reynolds seemed like the type who wouldn't pick up on it if I wanted him to.

"So how much farther until we get to this Cathedral of yours?"

"Ah, of course, it should present itself any moment!" He wasn't wrong, it made itself pretty damn apparent in a matter of seconds. The bellowing it made was almost like whalesong, dragging my attention to the little round windows. The Cathedral of Saint Gilbert, in all its haunting glory, drifted out of the clouds like a sweeper the size of a city. Its body was round, bloated beyond recognition, small hanging tendrils descended from its underside, twisting mindlessly in the breeze. Long, spindly arms and legs hung limp from it, webbed and paddle like. If it had been smaller I could imagine they'd aid in locomotion, but at its massive size I could only assume the bursts of gas from its numerous vents were the only thing moving it. The face was wide, bulging eyes glazed over, blinking slowly and slightly out of sync. Its mouth stretched in a yawning motion, emitting another burst of whalesong. I could only imagine its odour, worse even than the gas of its followers as they whizzed around it. Great spires, arches and buttresses lined its back, a vast cathedral, easily as big as any town or even city, all flesh-toned and seamlessly merged with its bulbous underside. "Isn't He magnificent?" Reynolds gushed, froggish face twisted in joy.

Not the word I'd have used, those were the words in my mind, but the ones that slid off my tongue were simple and not entirely untrue, "Yes," I nodded, "Yes, he is."

The little air-carriage landed moments later, and I was thankful for the chance to put a few more feet between myself and Father Reynolds. We touched down somewhere around the neck of the floating thing, a pair of enormous doors standing at the end of a long path in front of us. They seemed to be carved from bone, or had simply grown into this shape. The ground was cobbled with calluses, hard and sturdy on the skin of the thing. Reynolds hovered ahead, propelled by a stream of foul fumes that mingled with the emissions of the Cathedral. Following him to the door, I cursed myself for wasting the last of my ammo on Maxwell. The door creaked open, anticipating our approach.

"What is this place?" I finally worked up the nerve to ask as we crossed the threshold.

"The Cathedral of Saint Gilbert," Reynolds looked wistful, "As I said, He gave himself that we may have our own holy land, free from persecution." Looking at the organic architecture, the cattle-like mindlessness in the great floating thing's eyes, I was overcome with an unsettling feeling of what Reynolds may have meant by "*gave himself.*"

"Reynolds!" A familiar voice boomed, "Did you not think it wise to inform me of our guest's arrival?" The man from the phone, who I now saw before me. He was unlike the other Reconcilers, all pudgy and frog like. This man was long, slender, and angular. The lines of a scowl had eroded into the very structure of his face from years of sustaining the expression. He turned his gaze on me, revealing his almost completely white eyes. "I do apologize, Ms Rose. You didn't receive nearly the fanfare your arrival warrants."

"I don't need fanfare," I shook my head, clutching the canister under my arm, "I need answers, and I need my goddamn money."

"And you will get both, shortly. Please follow me." My feet worked with little input from me, dragging me in the path he followed, deeper into the flesh cathedral. "My name is-"

"I don't especially care."

"My name," he continued, "Is High Priest Voss. I am the fourth to occupy the title once held by our esteemed founder. I am also to be the first to truly achieve his vision."

"Yeah? And what vision would that be?"

"This one," he gestured to the wall, if a sheet of skin pulled taut between two pillars of bone could be called a wall. The light that streamed through was tinged red and painted the interior scarlet. All save for a patch, which was grown over with a translucent membrane, little blobs of colour that came together to form an image. Living stained glass. It depicted a scene of a man's body, split open, a shining dove emerging from it, and a crowd rejoicing.

"And what the hell am I supposed to make of that?" I uselessly gripped my hedgehog's handle, knowing if I needed it the best I could do would be pistol whip the priest. I rationalized that the stun baton would be better, but if the gas was flammable then things would go bad fast.

"Saint Gilbert believed that there was a need for meaning in the world. Objective meaning. He was also a strict materialist. He had no time for the notion that meaning could only be found in the mind, or in a book. He sought to reconcile these beliefs."

"And that involved being turned into a zeppelin?" I scoffed, drawing Voss' angry gaze.

"Saint Gilbert sought to create a material god, and came closer than any high priest since in ascending to his current form. Until now, of course." Voss snapped his fingers, a legion of Reconcilers descending on me suddenly, erupting from the walls and the floor, sopping with the cathedral's fluids. I was bound quickly, the canister rolling from me as my respirator was pulled away. I saw the faint yellow glow begin, then die out prematurely. One of the Reconcilers' throats ballooned, then a thick, blue smoke came from his vents, smothering me. Voss' voice was the last thing I heard before losing consciousness.

"Poor little thing," he held the canister in his hands, "He's tired himself out."

When I came to, I was handcuffed to something I could only describe as a rib. My arm was aching, pins and needles running along its length after being held above me so long. I struggled to get my feet under me, still dazed from the gas.

"Ah, you're awake," Voss smiled, "It's about time. I was worried we'd have to start the festivities without our honoured guest."

"Blow it out your ass."

"My, my, we'll have to strike that one from the texts. You're to be remembered as a saint, she who delivered The Larval God unto us. We can't have you remembered for your profanity."

"I repeat, blow it out your ass." I spat at him, a thick glob landing directly on his cheek. He snarled, wiping it away with his robe.

"You really are vermin, aren't you?"

"Want me to make it three times?"

"Such a waste. You had potential, you're almost pure. An implant in your neck, a bad pigment job," He sniffed the air, "A chromosomal sculpt. Nothing that deviates from human, even if you're a bit off your original design."

"How did you-" Being outed by smell alone was definitely a new experience, finally leaving me a little shaken.

"All mods leave a trace. Anyone who plays god gets an ego, they feel the need to sign their work. I've smelled sculpts like yours before, I do admire the initiative. I just wish you'd act the role a little better. Spitting at people," he leaned in close, "Not very ladylike." I sank my teeth into his nose, ripping it clean off. He dropped to the ground, howling in pain. His followers pulled an array of weapons on me.

"How's that for ladylike?"

"You… Bitch!"

"Ah, ah, Mr High Priest, must watch that profanity." His hands closed around my neck, slick with blood, seconds after I finished the sentence. I saw the inky tendrils of black seeping into the corners of my vision, closing in on Voss' bloody face. He let go as a golden glow erupted behind him, and stood.

"Aha," he cheered, kneeling before the canister. The armed priests dropped their weapons to follow suit. The tube was locked in place in some vast network of pipes. I got a good look around now, realizing this must be somewhere in the depths of the cathedral, within the beast. The pipes connected to an array of machines, pumps, generators, even what looked to be the exposed bones and blood vessels of the cathedral. It looked like life support. "Yes!" Voss screamed, "Yes, He is coming!" The glow grew brighter and brighter, cracks beginning to form in the canister's glass. The bald men all cheered in unison, all ecstatic to experience this moment, the moment of Reconciliation. A blinding light consumed us all, and the words of the cultists chilled me to the bone.

"God is born!"

Chapter Nineteen: Genesis

I had long since lost count of the number of times I'd feared for my life, but there had been four times I sincerely believed I was about to die. The first was the day a bird-headed man dragged me from the collapsed remnants of my home, caked in blood and dust with dozens of broken bones. The second was the day that same man was shot in front of me, and I ran like a coward with blood trailing from my shoulder and tens of armed men fully prepared to end my life. The third had only been a few hours ago, as I found myself falling into the blooming maw of a cancerous leviathan. The fourth moment was then and there, in the belly of Saint Gilbert, chained to its ribs, watching the biological nuke I'd carried for days finally detonate.

    The light was blinding, more so than when it had fended off the crabs, more than when it had rendered Maxwell a scorch mark in the oasis. This was something entirely new. Even through eyes clenched shut the light seared my retinas, casting shadows of the forms within. The light seemed to writhe and move but it was far too bright and vast for anything clear to be distinguished. A shadow emerged from where I assumed the canister had once been, a black ovoid thing I recognized as the maggot, the "Larval God" as Voss had described it. The shadow was impossibly dark, just like the creature's eyes had been. Less like a shadow and more like a hole carved in space, an emptiness. Its form warped and shifted, stretching in ways that didn't make sense for any three dimensional thing. Enormous void wings erupted from it, and even though it appeared to lack any volume I could tell that the hole had taken the shape of a colossal insect, easily three meters tall. Its wings flapped and the form contorted, growing thinner. Again, they flapped and the thing reshaped itself. Once again, and it was in the perfect shape of a man. All at once the shadow collapsed into an infinitesimal point, dragging its all-encompassing aura with it. By the time it had stopped receding, the shape of a man remained, now nothing but a blinding light. The wings unfurled again, radiant and speckled with eyespots of the perfect darkness. The brilliant thing cocked its head to the side, and the eyespots blinked.

"The pupation!" Voss hollered, "The pupation is complete, The Imago lives!" It turned its head to him, and Voss' head was rendered a fine red mist. It took his body a moment to register the absence, taking a step forward, arms outstretched, before dropping lifelessly to its knees. A pool of blood formed around it, barely distinct from the glistening red meat of the Cathedral. The other Reconcilers looked around, in silent awe at their leader being so unceremoniously ended by their newly ascended god.

"Dear god," Reynolds was the first to speak, drawing the gaze of the imago, "Why did-" There was nothing left of his head before he could complete the sentence. The others looked on, in shocked horror. Some froze, as if they sincerely believed it would do them any good. Others simply dropped in resignation, accepting their fate. The first to die were the ones who ran, simply evaporating mid-stride. The ones looking on in fear went next, then the ones who had resigned themselves. It had been less than ten seconds, in all, since the thing had burst from the canister. Ten seconds, and everyone in the room had died, everyone but me and their killer.

"You…" I struggled to get the words out as I pressed myself against the foul-smelling flesh of Saint Gilbert, "You killed them."

"I did." It spoke, its voice like a thousand swarming insects giving their best approximation of speech. "Are you alright?"

"I… Alright? You just killed-" I tried to tally up the bodies in my head but it quickly became apparent that I wouldn't need to.

"Forty two," it stated calmly, "Forty two in this room, along with the six hundred and twelve across the rest of the cathedral. I assure you, their deaths were painless, and if you knew the extent of their crimes you would insist I had been too merciful."

"What are you?"

"I am god." It stated plainly, in the same tone you might use to tell someone that the sky is blue or ice is cold.

"You're not god."

"They certainly seemed to think I was, until I killed them. At the very least, I am something like a god, easily mistaken for one."

"I don't know what the fuck you are, but you aren't a fucking god."

"I am god as much as a horse with a horn is a unicorn. I certainly fit the criteria."

"I'm… I'm not having this argument, you just killed-"

"Six hundred and fifty four."

"Six hundred and fifty four people! Is that something God would do?"

"Yes."

"I... Okay, fair point."

"Since you have failed to notice, I'll take this lull in the conversation to inform you that I have removed your bindings." I put my arm down, realizing suddenly that the imago had, in fact, removed the hand cuff.

"What do you want from me?"

"Why do you presume I want something from you?"

"Because I'm not a cloud of red mist right now."

"Fair point," the creature echoed my words, something in its tone giving the impression that it would be smirking if it had anything resembling a mouth. "You have taken me this far. You brought me here, to the site of my rebirth. I wish to thank you."

"What about them?" I gestured to the corpses that littered the floor. "They made you, why not thank them?"

"They made me so they could use me. They saw me as a tool, one to bring about their perfect utopia. I would have shown them mercy, had they not unleashed a serpent on their own Eden."

"Unleashed-"

"Maxwell," it cut me off, "It was no accident that he found you, or that he had been given his new form."

"But... Why? Why try to kill me?"

"I am all knowing, but I cannot profess to be all understanding. The minds of madmen are as much an enigma to me as to you. Perhaps they wished to weaken me, or test me, before I was allowed to ascend. Perhaps they simply wished to add some primordial beast to their creation myth. I cannot say."

"So… What now?"

"Now?" It spoke, with its hand outstretched, "I would like you to see something." I hesitantly accepted its hand, and found myself pulled into its radiance as if it was still the same hole in space it had been before the light filled it. When the light faded I was somewhere else, barren and rocky. Two moons hung in the sky like great eyes looking down over the landscape.

"Where are we?"

"Far away. Further than any man has tread, or likely ever will."

"You mean-"

"Yes."

"We're in outer-fucking-space!" It took me a second to hide the childlike excitement, a little embarrassed. "So… Why are we in outer-fucking-space?"

"You took on the duty to see me to my destination. This is my destination. I will not be returning."

"Oh."

"I have much I wish to do, and I'm afraid your world is too fragile, too precious, for me to stay."

"But… There's so much you could do, you could turn back ecological devastation, end poverty, explode corrupt politicians! You can't just… Leave!"

"It's true, earth has more than its fair share of problems, but I am not the solution. They are problems that require a fine tool and surgical precision. I am a blunt instrument. Where you need a scalpel, I am an atom bomb. Out here there is no one to harm. I am free to make the cosmos my canvas and fill it with meaning and purpose, but your people are so truly special. You can find meaning, make it, cultivate it. So when you leave here, you will never see me again. All I ask is that you find your meaning, and fulfil your purpose."

Beth's face flashed in my mind, then withered away to the image of her soft, pink brain laying in a tank. My heart sank as I realized there was no more Church of the Divine Reconciliation, and no money to treat her.

"The girl," the imago looked at me curiously, "She is your purpose?"

"My purpose, my meaning, the reason I get up every morning."

"Then take this," it pulled a briefcase from the blinding expanse within its chest and forced it into my arms, "Five million credits, exactly what the church had offered you. As their last surviving heir, I will pay their debt in full."

I was stunned, stammering for a moment before simply blurting out "Thank you."

"Now, may I examine your weapon?"

"My-" I was blindsided by the sudden turn, "My hedgehog?"

"Yes. You did not take me this far alone, I would like to extend my gratitude to the little one as well." I had barely even thought about it before handing her over. The thing's blinding face peered down into the hedgehog's single eye, which squinted at the harsh light. It blinked a few times, then the imago turned to me again. "She would like me to thank you."

"Thank- What?"

"For not letting Chroma dispose of her. She also wishes you'd stop calling her 'The Hedgehog.'"

"She... You can talk to her?"

"She lacks the capacity for language, she is more a visual thinker." I was at a loss for words, a little embarrassed that I'd never really considered my weapon's capacity for thought. One thing pushed its way through my crowded mind and off the tip of my tongue.

"What would she like to be called?"

"She prefers Cinder, or Cindy." The glowing thing pressed her into my palm and I looked her in the eye.

"Cindy, huh?" Her quilless follicles shivered gently, a look of joy crossing her eye.

"You should ask Chroma to help fit her with a tether link. You'll have a much easier time communicating over implants."

"I... I don't know what to say."

"I have one final gift. For Beth. You wouldn't have taken me this far without her. I would like you to give this to her." It pressed a little cube into my hand. "I trust you'll understand."

Eyeing it, there wasn't an ounce of hesitation in my mind. "I do."

"Excellent." It buzzed. "Then be on your way." With that, its blinding light engulfed me again, and without warning I was standing in the middle of a dusty warehouse.

"Tiff?" A feminine voice crackled behind me.

"Beth!" I spun around with joyful tears in my eyes.

Epilogue

Four months had passed since the collapse of the Church of the Divine Reconciliation. In that time, I had barely heard Beth's voice, but the day had finally arrived. I sat in the vast, dark expanse of the mindscape, passing time until I would get to see her. The neuroplastic tether in my neck produced a distinct pop as the other end connected and a figure appeared in the distance. I walked up to her, slowly. A little girl, unnaturally white with messy, maroon hair. She wore a pair of denim overalls, her hands stuffed in the pockets.

"Cinder?" I asked. She turned to look at me, one eye covered by her fringe. She nodded slowly, unsure of how to properly maneuver her avatar in this space. Her mouth stretched into a smile, looking a little unnatural though that could be put down to the lack of practice.

"It's good to see you, in… Person?"

She nodded again, confirming for me that I'd chosen the right phrase.

"I don't really know-" The mute little girl caught me off guard by wrapping her arms around me, pulling me into a hug and almost tackling me to the ground in the process. I patted her on the head, laughing. "You've been waiting a long time for that, huh?" She nodded, giggling silently. She pulled away, raising a finger to gesture for me to wait. She reached around in her pockets and pulled out a crumpled piece of paper, forcing it into my hands. It was a crude drawing of three figures. A tall woman with black hair, bar a single streak of white. A little girl with one eye and spiky hair. A jar with a brain inside, sitting on top of a little cabinet. The girl had a big grin on her face.

"It's adorable," I smiled, "I'll take it to hypnoprint and get a copy to carry around." Cindy flailed her hands in non-verbal glee, then pulled the picture down towards her and pointed to the jar. "Beth?" I asked, and she nodded vigorously, "Yeah, today's the day. You ready to go see her?" She nodded again. "We'll have to plug out," I clarified. Cindy frowned a little, then wrapped her small arms around my waist. She looked up to me and nodded.

The tether detached from my neck, and I pulled the other end from the freshly healed implant on Cindy's grip. I smiled at her before gently placing her in her holster. I mounted the new bike, replaced after Maxwell's mutated form crushed the last one, and sped off toward the warehouse Frankie had so graciously loaned out to us for the procedure. Inside Frankie greeted me casually, and excitedly.

"I'm so happy to see her again! Four months is entirely too long!"

"How do you think I feel?" I laughed. "Are they in there?"

"Yeah, I don't think they've slept for days, been tending to her around the clock."

"And it's definitely today?"

"Doc says so, a matter of hours at most."

"Thank god." I pushed ahead, Frankie following behind into the main area of the warehouse. A huge, pinkish pod sat in the centre, hooked up to all manner of wires and tubes. I could see her outline through its translucent flesh. The artificial womb was growing a whole new body around Beth.

"Ah, you're here, I was beginning to worry you'd be late." Chroma snarked, slithering up behind me. I clutched the little cube from the imago tight.

"I wouldn't miss this for the world." I sat expectantly in the rusted old folding chair that sat in front of the massive pod, thinking back on everything I'd seen and done. One night stuck out, more than all the gods and monsters. The carnival. The overpowering smell of candy, the sounds of children, happy, laughing children. It was a rare thing these days. I held Beth's hand, smelled her lavender perfume mixed with the faint traces of perspiration accumulated from running from ride to ride. We looked out over the world, sitting on top of the ferris wheel. She looked down at the lights, the joy, the music, but I couldn't take my eyes off her. How the lights bounced off her hair, the technicolor mess casting her face in a million strobing shades. Her lips, bright red. I put my hand on her cheek and turned her to look at me. There, on top of the world, I kissed her. Then I told her I loved her for the first time, and she smiled. "I love you too."

The pod shuddered, then ruptured, and I stood bolt upright as Beth spilled to the ground in the puddle of amniotic fluid. She coughed up the slime from her lungs, awkwardly adjusting herself around her newfound umbilical cord. I knelt down beside her and helped her up to eye level. She looked at me, dripping with viscous orange slime, pink and hairless, and her eyelids fluttered, and she was as beautiful as she'd ever been.

"Hey, stranger," she cracked a smile, the first smile on a new, familiar face. I ran a finger along her cheek, remembering the long indentation that she had on it before, from a fight with some drunken sailors, she'd told me.

"I'm gonna miss that scar," I laughed.

"Me too, it made me look tough," we both broke into a fit of giggles, then her lips pressed to mine. I pulled back, still smiling.

"I did it."

"You did it?"

"I killed Maxwell."

"I'm proud of you," she kissed me again, her lips wet with the thick fluid of the artificial womb.

"I-" I pulled myself away again, "I have something I want to ask you."

"You do?" She smiled, that same beautiful smile that made my heart melt. I pulled the little box the imago had given me from my pocket and opened it.

"Bethany Franklin, will you marry me?"